BELOVED TORMENTOR

SARAH FRASER

THORNDIKE
CHIVERS

This Large Print edition is published by Thorndike Press, Waterville, Maine, USA and by BBC Audiobooks Ltd, Bath, England.
Thorndike Press is an imprint of Thomson Gale, a part of The Thomson Corporation.
Thorndike is a trademark and used herein under license.

LIBRARY OF CONGRESS CATALOGING-IN-PUBLICATION DATA

Fraser, Sarah.
  Beloved tormentor / by Sarah Fraser. — Large print ed.
    p. cm. — (Thorndike press large print candlelight)
  ISBN-13: 978-0-7862-9573-9 (alk. paper)
  ISBN-10: 0-7862-9573-2 (alk. paper)
  1. Large type books. I. Title.
PS3606.R424B45 2007
813'.6—dc22   2007010886

BRITISH LIBRARY CATALOGUING-IN-PUBLICATION DATA AVAILABLE

Published in 2007 in the U.S. by arrangement with Robert Hale Limited.
Published in 2007 in the U.K. by arrangement with Robert Hale Limited.

U.K. Hardcover: 978 1 405 64090 9 (Chivers Large Print)
U.K. Softcover: 978 1 405 64091 6 (Camden Large Print)

Printed in the United States of America on permanent paper
10 9 8 7 6 5 4 3 2 1

BELOVED TORMENTOR

ONE

As the taxi drove smoothly out of Edinburgh Airport and towards the elegant capital, Julia wondered yet again if life were playing an elaborate hoax on her. It had all happened so quickly that she had barely had time for questions or doubts. Only ten days ago she had been in Paris finalising two years of research for Madame de Poulange's latest historical novel. Now, she was on the last stretch of an expenses-paid trip to Edinburgh, to be interviewed for a job so vaguely described as 'very special assistant'. It sounded, and felt, quite unreal.

It was, nevertheless, very flattering to be treated like a VIP — especially since she might turn out to be totally unsuited to the job. Obviously, Madame's recommendation had carried some weight with her old school friend, Barbara, Lady Muirisson.

It had always been understood that Julia's stay with Madame de Poulange would end when research for the book was completed and, although Julia had been invited to stay on as long as she wished, she was ready for a change. Her only qualm at leaving had been the difficulty of finding a new post which was equally challenging. Madame, who had grown very fond of Julia in the two years since her arrival, newly graduated, in Paris, had immediately sprung into action with the help of her social 'grapevine' and, as a result, Julia had been offered this interview.

As the taxi reached the outskirts of the capital, Julia's nervousness increased. Supposing she was offered this mysterious job — should she take it? She had loved her work in Paris, and the life she had led there. Was a castle on a Scottish island likely to be an anti-climax? She had always enjoyed a challenge but, knowing so little about this job, she felt uncertain, and rather embarrassed at the amount of trouble taken over her.

She paid the taxi-driver and hesitated outside the imposing hotel as the porter carried in her luggage. It was good to be back in Edinburgh, where she had been a student for four years. She gazed down the busy length of Princes Street, and up towards the rocky bulk of Castle Rock. What a lovely city this was!

In the hotel foyer she was greeted by the receptionist. "Miss Markman? Welcome to Edinburgh! I'm afraid Mr Muirisson is out at the moment, but he has left a message for you." It seemed that Lady Muirisson was unwell and had not been able to make the trip. Her son was keeping one of the business appointments she had made. However, he hoped that Julia would enjoy afternoon tea here, and meet him for dinner at 8 p.m.

As her 'butterflies' subsided, Julia decided she was quite glad of the opportunity to relax after her trip. In her room she hung up her clothes and freshened up. At least, she thought as she surveyed herself in the mirror, her appearance hadn't suffered from the journey. She had swept her rich auburn hair back from her face into a chignon, which she hoped looked attractive and suitable for an efficient assistant. Nervousness had brought a slight flush to her high cheekbones, emphasising the green of her eyes. Her smartly-cut suit would hardly do for dinner, and she was glad that she had brought the dress Madame had chosen as her parting gift.

She collected her thoughts over tea. She had been surprised at first by the name 'Mr

Muirisson' until she remembered that Lady Barbara had a younger son. Madame had spent some time giving her some 'background' on the family. Lady Muirisson had been widowed six months ago and death duties had made her decide to open Berristane Castle to the public in an attempt to avoid selling. It was in connection with this project that she needed an assistant. The heir to the title, Michael, had not met with Madame's approval. It seemed that Julia was the only person in Europe who hadn't heard tell of the playboy aristocrat. A rebel of sorts, he had lived away from home during the fifteen years since his coming of age. He had been a successful if daredevil racing driver for a small British manufacturer until a serious accident, ironically as a passenger in a friend's car, several weeks after his father's death. He was known as a jet-setter, a rather flamboyant character who enjoyed his reputation as a 'ladykiller'. Julia, never one to be impressed by the 'in crowd' lifestyle, had never read the 'gossip' magazines which Madame perused so thoroughly, and Michael's history was of little interest to her.

"Young Robert is quite different however!" her employer had enthused. "You will like him, cherie, he is the true gentleman!" Her report of the younger Muirisson was so glowing, that Julia suspected exaggeration! Now, it seemed, she would be able to judge for herself.

Naively delighted by the luxurious surroundings of the hotel, Julia whiled away the hours before dinner, bathing and washing her hair at a leisurely pace. This, she reflected, could be her reward for surviving the last two frantic weeks. It was sheer enjoyment to pamper herself, and she wanted to look her best for her prospective employer.

She applied her make-up with extra care, pleased that she needed so little help from brushes and pots! She allowed her gleaming hair to fall loose to her shoulders, a style which suited the black silk jersey dress from the Paris coutourier. As she checked herself over in the cheval glass, she noted with satisfaction how flattering the cut of the expensive dress was to her slim but shapely figure. Yes, she decided, she felt wonderful! And even if she did not get the job, this was a most enjoyable experience.

Her earlier nervousness quite dispelled by her relaxed afternoon, Julia made her way down to the French Dining Room suggested by Mr Muirisson. She was shown to a table for two in the deep bay of a window overlooking Princes Street Gardens and the floodlit elegance of the city's famous buildings. The dining room itself was gently lit, its heavy velvet drapes and embossed wall coverings creating a sophisticated but intimate atmosphere. She smiled to herself; this was not a typical interview room!

At that moment a young man entered the room, rubbing his hands briskly as though coming in out of the cold. Robert Muirisson was about Julia's age, tall and broad-shouldered, with a wide smile, freckles and a shock of red hair. He looked almost out of place in the studied elegance of the lush dining room. As he strode towards the table he extended both hands to shake hers in a welcome of genuine warmth.

"I'm so sorry for the delay!" he exclaimed. "Mother wasn't able to come along because of the 'flu, and I've been trying to keep her appointments as well as my own. It's been rather hectic!" His eyes sparkled with good humour. "I don't suppose you should say 'I'm starving!' in such elegant surroundings, but I am! Shall we enjoy our meal and get to know each other first, before we get down to business?" Julia readily agreed, and as the mouthwatering courses followed one another, she had to agree with Robert that the chef was indeed a genius!

Madame, Julia soon decided, had not been wearing rose-tinted specs. Robert was indeed charming, polite, and obviously interested to meet her. She had never been 'interviewed' in a more unusual manner. Robert made her feel at ease from the start.

As they waited for coffee and Robert's Tia Maria, he sat back and looked at her with disarming frankness. "Now," he asked. "What would you like to know about us?"

"I'm sorry?" Julia could not catch his meaning.

"Well, Miss Markman — Julia — Annis de Poulange's references were so glowing that my mother needed no more convincing that you were our girl — if you'll forgive the expression! So really it's more a matter of your interviewing me!"

Julia laughed shyly. It was very flattering to be treated like this, but what could she say? "I . . ." she hesitated. Understanding her embarrassment Robert launched into a description of the job which was being offered.

In several weeks time, at the beginning of June, Berristane Castle would be opened to the public. There would be guided tours of the major public rooms, with treasures dating back many centuries, the grounds and gardens would be open to visitors, and various publicity events from musical evenings to nature rambles would be organised.

All this was causing a massive upheaval in the household. The family would live in the castle's west-wing, which had stood empty for several years. It was now being converted into apartments, and Lady Barbara had to supervise builders and craftsmen, as well as planning decor, and ordering furnishings.

"I'm often away on the mainland on estate business, and Mother must have permanent help with all the work involved. We need someone to co-ordinate, and double-check all the things which are happening. Truly — we do hope you'll take us on!" He paused, and then, as though he felt uneasy about what he had to say, he continued slowly. "As you may know, my brother Michael has had to give up motor racing after a road crash. At the moment he's in the Caribbean, a sort of long convalescence, but we do expect him home soon. We haven't seen him since just after the accident . . ." He explained that Michael, although heir to the title, had never been greatly interested in the castle and the estate. Of course Julia knew this from Madame's potted biography. It would hardly have suited his trendy image to be trudging around farms in green wellies!

Robert looked apologetic. "If you have any doubts, of course . . ." Julia thought it strange that the mention of Michael might be expected to raise such doubts. Her natural impulse was to say 'yes' immediately. She trusted Robert's honesty and, although she was not attracted to him, he seemed a super person and a potential friend. Madame de Poulange's description of her friend Barbara had been enchanting, and the job itself sounded so challenging! What more could she ask? Just as she was about to give her answer, Robert spoke again. "Look — you've had a long day and I'm rushing you! Why don't you meet me for breakfast — say 9 a.m. — and you can give me your decision then." He really was the soul of tact.

Julia was grateful to him for allowing her time to mull over all that he had said. As she prepared for bed she was filled with excitement. How could she turn down such an opportunity? History had been her subject at University, and Berristane was well known for the number and variety of its treasures. To help the family share these treasures with the island's many visitors, to be part of a new venture, to meet such a fascinating family — yes, even the apparently awe-inspiring Michael — was a wonderful prospect!

She slipped between the cool sheets expecting difficulty in falling asleep but, as Robert had said, it had been a long day, and soon her eyelids grew deliciously heavy.

She was awakened the following morning by the chambermaid bringing her coffee, and after showering and dressing she went downstairs to meet Robert. When he caught sight of her he leaped up to hold the chair for her, his warm smile now familiar. He was eager to hear her decision, and when she told him she accepted the post, was filled with childlike glee.

"I must 'phone Mother after breakfast! This will be such a weight off her mind! And I'm so pleased that you've agreed. I think we're going to be really good friends."

"When would you like me to start?" Julia asked. "I only need a few days in London to pack and buy some new clothes."

"Yes — a few winter woollies wouldn't go wrong — even for summer! Mind you, we have some marvellous weather too. Did you know we have palm trees?" He was ready to launch into a description of his beloved island, when he realised that he had not answered Julia's query.

"Well, how about Monday for travelling? There are several ferries and we can arrange

16

to have someone to meet you. We can fina-
lise the arrangements after breakfast if you
like!" His boyish lightheartedness was infec-
tious and Julia found herself wishing that
he did not have to leave so soon. However,
she had decided to spend a few hours in
Edinburgh before her flight back to London,
and she was looking forward to revisiting
some of her old haunts. She said goodbye
to Robert after completing arrangements
for her arrival on the island, and went
upstairs to gather her belongings.

Over the next few days she had little time
to mull over any doubts which might have
arisen; there was simply too much to cram
into such a short time. Aunt Liz, with whom
Julia had lived after her parents' death, was
delighted to see her niece so happy, but a
little sceptical of the benefits of life on a
Scottish island!

"Well, dear, it doesn't seem too far from
land," she declared reassuringly, as she
pored over a map of Scotland. "But I should
think it will be . . ." she searched for the
correct word ". . . bracing. And you'd better
stock up on clothes and books; and perhaps
a few packets of soup, some biscuits . . ."

"Oh, Mum! It's not the Polar Ice-cap!"
laughed Julia's cousin, Anne. "They do have
shops, you know! They've even heard of

electricity!" She and Julia stifled their giggles as Aunt Liz glared at them.

"Well . . . it's up to you, of course! But I'd take plenty of vests . . ." Julia surrendered to hilarity as Anne added, "And what about a liberty bodice?"

On the evening before her departure, Julia and Anne sorted through and packed all the new clothes she had bought — warm woollens, hats, gloves, good wellies and sturdy shoes; and an assortment of outfits which might suit the many aspects of her new job. Julia had never bought an entire 'wardrobe' before and she had found it exciting to have a real spree in London's best stores.

"It's been a bit like gathering a trousseau!" said Anne, and undeterred by Julia's warning grimace she went on: "Well — you never know! Two eligible men, landed gentry to boot! Of course I suppose the Scotsman may not be so sophisticated as the Frenchman . . ." She dived for cover as Julia aimed a cushion at her.

"Honestly, you're as bad as Aunt Liz. My career is my priority just now, not catching a husband!" Aware that she sounded a bit abrasive, she smiled at Anne. "Anyway, Robert's sweet and kind, but he's not my type, romantically speaking."

"But what about the other one?" Anne pursued.

"Well — I suppose he sounds interesting. But I've never found spoiled rich kids very attractive and that's what he seems to be! I suppose I should feel sorry for him, after his accident." Her voice trailed off. "Anyway — I shouldn't think we'll see much of him." But as they closed and locked her suitcases and made final preparations, Julia's thoughts kept returning to Lord Michael. Why had Madame been so merciless in her criticism of him? Why had Robert been so uneasy about mentioning him? And did they really think Michael would leave his jet-set cronies to settle down on a Scottish isle, even if he now owned a chunk of it?

But she had put these queries aside by the time her flight landed at Glasgow Airport the following morning. She stepped out into a crisp, clear spring day, the perfect weather for her drive north. The rental car was waiting and Julia set off, filled with a sense of adventure, on the next stage of her journey.

She had studied the road maps carefully, but after the first few miles north through the heavily-populated, industrial belt, there was little need to refer to them. Gradually, motorways and by-passes were left behind as she skirted the famous shores of Loch

Lomond; and soaring on her right the grandeur of Ben Lomond, still capped with snow.

Julia's mother had been a Scot and although she had not visited this area since childhood, Julia felt a strange sense of homecoming in the ruggedness of the landscape.

After Arrochar, she headed westwards to the harbour town of Finnsport. Cresting the final hill before descending to the sea, she caught her breath at the sight before her, and drew in to the roadside to take it in.

In the distance, set in a sea beaten pale gold by the spring sun, lay the Isle of Rosa, its jagged mountain peaks defiant against a crystal blue sky. Julia felt a sudden rush of emotion at the beauty of it! This magical island was to be 'home' to her now.

Despite the keen sea breeze, she spent the latter half of the ferry crossing up on deck, her face lifted towards the beckoning isle. Gradually, aspects of its landscape became clearer, hillsides, forests, fields, villages formed themselves against the backdrop of the island's bulky shape. It was truly breathtaking, and she was so absorbed in the view that she almost forgot why she was coming to Rosa.

At last, the Captain's voice instructed

vehicle owners to make their way to the car deck, and the few other passengers began to collect their belongings. Julia decided that she would need two trips to carry off her cases, but when the gangway was in place, Robert bounded on to the ferry and greeted her with his usual warmth. Loading himself with cases, he shepherded her down on to the pier.

"The car's just along here," he called, as Julia paused to take in her surroundings. "You're very quiet. Has Rosa captured you already?"

"She laughed. "Yes — Yes. I think it has. It's even more magical than you suggested." She became increasingly bewitched by the island's beauty as Robert's Range Rover carried them the few miles to Berristane. Every bend in the winding coastal road unveiled another dramatic seascape, or hillside, and in the deepening twilight Ben Tarag loomed over them.

As the car turned through high, wrought-iron gates and up a tree-lined driveway, Julia suddenly felt nervous. This was it! Her instinct for adventure had brought her this far, and there was no turning back. But if anything could have been guaranteed to dispel these nerves it was Robert's cheery "Here we are, then! Home at last!" Leaving staff to attend to Julia's luggage, he led her along narrow corridors, past huge drums of paint, and stepladders, dust-sheeted furniture and joiners' tools until he opened a freshly-painted door marked 'Private. Not open to the Public.'

"Mother's like a dog with two tails!" he laughed. "At long last she's shooed the builders and decorators out of this wing and she's revelling in getting the rooms just to her liking." The newly renovated hallway and staircase were certainly impressive, and the bright, airy room into which Robert now led her combined grace with warmth and cheeriness.

"Ah, Miss Markman! Welcome to Berristane!" The tall, slim woman who crossed the lounge to meet Julia was certainly not the elderly duchess one might have expected. At sixty, Lady Barbara retained a youthful glow in her appearance, her style of dress, and her effortlessly elegant manner. "You must be quite exhausted after your long journey! Do sit down for a while and rest. We've held back dinner until 8.30 to allow you time to change and 'unwind' a little."

The conversation was relaxed and interesting. Lady Barbara shared anecdotes of the horrors caused by the conversion work, and expressed genuine delight and relief at having 'found' Julia to help her. However, as she talked of the work still to be done in such a short time, and the endless small details which required attention, it was clear to Julia that her employer was a woman who thrived on such excitement. It would be fun to work for her.

Over dinner, Lady Barbara described Julia's duties in more detail. The rooms which were to be opened to the public were now decorated and furniture which was being restored and cleaned by mainland specialists would soon be returned. The wide range of treasures and collections, and the many paintings, would need to be rearranged to best advantage. This was to be Julia's first priority.

"However," added Lady Barbara, "tomorrow you must be free to become acquainted with the castle and grounds. There is a great deal to see. And you'll find our library very helpful when it comes to the history of Rosa and of the castle."

Julia retired early to unpack and recover from her day's travelling. Her rooms were delightful, high-ceilinged with dormer windows overlooking the castle grounds. The bedroom was decorated in pale pastels, with beautiful rosewood furnishings, and her sittingroom included a working area with desk, filing cabinet, phone and typewriter. She was filled with enthusiasm for the job to be tackled and had it not been for the effects of Rosa's fine Scots air, she might have made a start then and there.

Robert was already out on the estate when Julia finished breakfast the following morning, and his mother was busy talking to her accountant. Donning boots and a warm jacket, Julia set off towards the gardens. Even at this time of year, with only spring flowers in bloom in the beds, the walled garden was impressive, with banks of brilliant gold and orange gorse against its walls. As she strolled along the pathways, she marvelled at the amount of dedicated work evident in the way the gardens were kept.

"Morning, Miss!" An elderly man was kneeling by one of the flower beds, trowel in hand. "You'll be our new lass — to help Lady B?" His weatherbeaten face creased in a broad smile. "My name's Mackenzie — gardener and chief blether — or 'gossip' to you!"

"Well, a newcomer's always glad of a bit of a — 'blether'," Julia smiled. "I've got such a lot to learn about this place!"

"Och, you'll have no bother, lass! And Lady B and that young Robert'll be a fine help. Good thing the other one's not here yet, though. I doubt he'd be enough to frighten you away!"

Julia was fascinated. Did no-one have a good word to say about Michael? As though sensing her thoughts, the old man went on, "Oh he was a nice enough wee boy, but since he left home — all that high-flying nonsense, and the fancy friends! Too good-looking, my wife's always said, and he knew it too! A right ladies' man, I've heard." It became clear that, in Mackenzie's opinion, the estate was better off without its lord and master.

As Julia said goodbye and moved on, out of the garden, she smiled at the gardener's ability to pass on so much information in such a short time! A useful friend!

By the time she returned to the castle Julia was entranced with Berristane. Set in to the hillside and sheltered by trees of many varieties, it looked out over a wide bay towards Rosa's mountain peaks. Every way you turned, the view was breathtaking. It was little wonder that holidaymakers so loved this island.

As she wandered through the castle's wood-panelled hallway, she gazed with interest at the family portraits hung there. Some were very old, the magnificent figures dressed in wigs, doublet and hose; the women laden with heavy brocades and jewels. Then, as she ascended the stairs, the portraits and their subjects became more modern until she stopped on the landing under a fine portrait of a tall, elegant man with red hair, dressed in army dress uniform. This was Robert's father, the late Duke. How wonderful, Julia thought, to be able to trace your family's history through several hundred years, simply by climbing a staircase.

She turned to climb the remaining few steps and was stopped in her tracks. At the top of the staircase, above a magnificent sideboard, there hung a portrait of a young man in casual clothes, painted against a background of Rosa's mountains. Even on canvas he looked physically overwhelming, his confidence — arrogance, perhaps — stated in his defiant stance. But it was the face which made her reach for the newel-post as though to steady herself. Blazing blue eyes seemed to look straight at her; the smile mocked the watcher. This was simply the most beautiful male face she had ever seen. The deep auburn hair swept away from the broad forehead, the cheekbones were high, like the old Duke's, and the lips full and sensually curved. Julia shook her head in amazement: perhaps this was a very flattering portrait. She was startled by the voice at her side.

"Michael draws another admirer!" Robert's tone did not sound as lighthearted as he might have intended. Julia noted a trace of unfamiliar bitterness which quite shocked her. "Even the painter found him 'challenging'! In fact she probably fell for him!"

"She . . . ? Oh, well perhaps it's idealised?"

"No, no I must admit it did him justice. If anything, Michael was even more handsome."

"Was?" Julia found use of the past tense rather eerie.

"Julia, my brother's crash left him with scarring to his face. We haven't seen him since the bandages were removed — he refused to see anyone. But we were told by his doctor that he is very, very self-conscious about it — he was rather vain about his appearance, you see. In fact, he seems more concerned with the facial scarring than with his leg injury. Mother thinks the Caribbean holiday has been his way of hiding from us, and from himself. I'm afraid we just don't know what to expect when he comes home."

Julia felt cold suddenly. She was shocked, hurt even, that such a wonderful face should be marred. She looked up at the portrait again and her heart turned over. Embarrassed, and aware that Robert could sense the strength of her reaction, she started on up the stairs. Robert grasped her arm almost roughly, so that she had to stop and turn back to him.

"Julia — you're a lovely person, and a beautiful young woman, and we're so happy to have you with us. Please — when Michael arrives — be careful!"

"I don't understand . . ."

"My brother is a very attractive man. He has a powerful personality and an immense amount of energy. He dominates relationships — you always live in his shadow if you know him, and especially if you love him." Robert's voice faltered. "And with the emotional effects of his accident . . . just, take care, Julia." He passed her abruptly and went briskly up the stairs, turning away down one of the corridors.

Julia drew in her breath. What kind of man was Michael to have everyone so terrified of him? Why did they surrender to his dominant will? Attractive he might be — incredibly so — but she, for one, would not allow herself to be overwhelmed by his, or any man's, personality!

TWO

Julia was amazed at the speed and ease with which she settled in to life at Berristane. The island's quite magical spell had captured her from the first, and it was hard not to feel at home in the company of her new employers and the staff who so happily worked for them.

So it was with some resentment that she heard news, several weeks later, of Michael's imminent arrival. Although they rarely discussed him, Lady Barbara and her younger son had seemed uneasy, nervous almost, at the mention of his name in conversation. Despite herself, Julia was fascinated.

Michael was due to arrive on the morning ferry, and had asked that only Robert should meet him at the pier.

"I assume he'll have piles of luggage!" Lady Barbara explained to Julia. "So he'll need Bob to help with the lifting and loading! I wouldn't be much use at all!" She laughed nervously. "I'll just have to play 'mother hen' here until he comes, and put some finishing touches to his room. Perhaps, my dear, you could see Mackenzie for me — have some fresh blooms sent up." Her lovely face was flushed, and her manner rather distracted. Julia, who had grown very fond of her sweet-natured yet strong employer, felt concerned for her. There seemed something vulnerable in Lady Barbara's excitement at the prospect of welcoming home her first-born; Julia felt protective towards her.

She was working in the Blue Drawing Room that morning, casting an eye over the final placing of the exquisite furniture and checking the information sheets compiled for the castle guides, and she had hoped that Lady Barbara might join her, even briefly. But as she stood by the tall casement windows with their breathtaking view of the gardens, and the wide sweep of the bay beyond, she could see the elegant figure walking — or rather, pacing — the terrace in front of the main door and at that moment, as the ferry nosed into sight, heading towards the distant pier, Julia too was overwhelmed by a feeling of anticipation. What a man, indeed, to have so many people awaiting his arrival as though he were Royalty!

Despite the general air of excitement, however, it was impossible for her not to become quickly absorbed in her work. What a privilege it was to work here! The visitors who would soon pass through this room would 'ooh!' and 'aah!' from behind rope barriers, but here she was actually holding in her hand a piece of the most delicate Sèvres porcelain, a figure of an innocent girl in a white gown. It was perfection!

Her calm was disturbed by one of the staff, Jenny, appearing at the door. "Miss? It's Mr Robert, Miss. Asking for you in the library," and added guiltily, "He seems awfully flustered, Miss!"

"Tell him I'll be there in a moment, Jenny!" Julia answered, and reading the girl's blushes as a guide to Robert's state of mind, she hastily gathered her papers and catalogues together and with a few parting instructions to the two girls working in the next door bed chamber, she hurried to the library.

Robert was pouring coffee as she entered, with a deliberateness which suggested that he was forcing himself to keep calm. Before she could speak he launched into a tirade which seemed quite out of character.

"That damned, arrogant brother of mine! Do you know —" he was rapidly losing any pretence of control over his fury. "Would you believe that after all this time, after the accident, after refusing to let us near him, knowing — surely he must know — what Mother has been through, he arrives here and announces that he doesn't intend to stay in the castle!"

"I'm sorry . . . ?" Julia found it hard to follow this stream of words, and Robert, stopping for breath, again struggled to compose himself.

"I met the ferry. There he was, porters rushing about, carrying bags and cases off for him, the lord and master! He could hardly bring himself to speak to me and then — just as we approached the gates he announced that he had decided to stay at the Lodge! 'More sensible,' says he. Never a thought for Mother, of course! It's just a damn good job I had a key on me or I'd probably have been sent off like a message-boy to fetch it, on a silken cushion!" He sat down heavily in the great armchair, his face still white with anger.

Julia had seen the Lodge house on her exploration of the grounds and was surprised that it was habitable.

"Oh, it's in reasonable repair," said Robert, "but barely a stick of furniture, and hardly, I would have thought, to Lord Michael's taste!" Julia was saddened by the bitterness aroused in her friend by his brother's behaviour.

Lady Barbara, naturally, had been deeply hurt by her son. Although she could almost understand Michael's desire for privacy, his refusal at least to come to the castle to greet her had left her upset and bewildered, and she had gone to her rooms, leaving instructions that she was not to be disturbed.

"I'm afraid I have a favour to ask of you, Julia," Robert explained now, calmer at last. "He wants someone to drive down to the Lodge with some books, and small items of furniture from his rooms here. I hope it doesn't seem to be pushing you in at the deep end, but he's obviously determined to steer clear of his family, if possible!"

The Range Rover had been packed with items listed by Michael, and after a lunch barely touched by her or Robert, Julia set off to the Lodge. As she turned the ignition she realised that her hands were trembling, and suddenly she was filled with anger at this man who had so upset people she cared for, and seemed to be having the same effect on her before she had even met him. She refused to be browbeaten like this! As she drew up outside the Lodge, she pulled on the handbrake with an aggressiveness designed to give her confidence. Taking a deep breath, she began to unload the first packages from the front seat.

There was no reply to her knocking and, staggering under the weight of her packages, she finally pushed gently on the door. It swung open, and stepping hesitantly inside she called out. "Hello? Sir?" There was no reply and the boxes seemed ready to fall. She bent to let them tumble on to the polished floor, and as she straightened up, rubbing her aching back, she suveyed the room. It was chaotic: some items of furniture were still covered by dust sheets; bags and fine leather luggage were strewn about; there was a heap of wood ash in the huge stone fireplace, and old newspapers were scattered around the ingle. And yet, untidy though it was, the room seemed to possess some strange power, an atmosphere of which she was immediately aware.

She was pondering whether she should struggle to bring in the remaining boxes herself, or leave well alone and return later, when a door opened and a man walked in, at first oblivious to her presence.

"Who the hell are you?" he demanded, suddenly noticing her presence. Julia was taken aback by his rudeness, but what really robbed her of speech was his face. She had prepared herself to avoid staring at Michael's face, expecting ugliness where there had once been beauty. But the face before her now, with only a purple line from the side of the nose running up and along the cheekbone, was even more attractive than the portrait on the staircase.

The slightly-feminine perfection had been replaced by a kind of fierce animal energy. He was simply the most powerfully attractive man she had ever seen.

"I'm Julia Markman," she stammered, tearing her eyes from his face but not, perhaps, before he had noticed and misunderstood her stare. "Your mother has hired me as her . . ."

"Where's the rest of my stuff?" he interrupted, obviously quite uninterested in what she had to say, or who she was. Born gentleman or not, he had the arrogance of a dictator!

Her heart pounding, with anger and some other emotion she refused to accept, she told him very coolly that the Range Rover was piled high, not only with the items he had requested, but with food and drinks and little extras his mother had thought of.

"Oh, trust Mother to think of all my

comforts!" he exclaimed sarcastically and as he moved past her towards the door Julia noticed how pronounced was the limp Robert had told her of. Sympathy flooded over her and, feeling that he must be in pain, she went outside after him. "I can carry these in for you . . ." she began and immediately saw that she had said quite the wrong thing. He whirled round, his magnificent features clenched with fury.

"I may be injured, Miss Markman, but I am not a cripple! I don't need a woman — you, or my mother — to treat me as though I were! I think we had better get that straight here and now!"

Julia's embarrassment forced her into silence and she stood by the car, watching him make his way back and forward many times, his face set in a determined grimace. He had been inexcusably rude to her and, more important, to his poor mother, who had not seen him since his accident and was ill with worry at his strange behaviour. But the emotion Julia felt was not anger.

As he lifted the last box she ventured to speak. "Your mother asked if she might come down this evening to see you. I think she feels . . ."

Yet again, he interrupted her words. "Tell her to leave it 'til tomorrow morning. I've

36

far too much sorting out to do today. And find out who on this island can fit an electric shower in this place, will you?"

He turned away from her, but the box he was carrying was much heavier than he had expected and, wincing as he twisted on his damaged leg, he stumbled. Julia automatically reached to help him, her hands grasping his arm, and for one brief moment his body seemed almost to welcome her support: his eyes met hers, and she was appalled at the pain she saw there! This man's agony was more than physical, she realised, shocked at the nakedness of his pain. But the moment was past; he wrenched away from her and disappeared into the Lodge.

As she drove back towards the castle, the remembered expression in his eyes overwhelmed any other emotion she might have experienced. Here was a man in hiding from a family who loved him. He was domineering, handsome, rude, arrogant, apparently contemptuous of women, and yet in one unguarded moment had revealed to her, a stranger, his pain. She was in turmoil, unable to control her confusion; no man she had met in her life had ever drawn her as he did, and yet she had thought him in so many ways the kind of man she despised.

Robert came out of the main door as she

drew up in front of the castle. He seemed anxious. "Well?" he asked.

Julia laughed. "Fine friend you are! Talk about into the lion's den!" Seeing Robert's stricken look she relented. "Oh, it wasn't that bad, really. But he obviously took an instant dislike to me — and I have to admit I wasn't exactly charmed myself!" Even as she said the words, trying to cheer Robert up, she knew that her reaction to Michael was so complex that she could never have explained it, perhaps not even to herself.

Lady Barbara accepted her son's postponed invitation with a quiet smile. She was quite calm now, and apparently resigned to Michael's decision to live at the Lodge. She certainly showed no signs of being the mother hen Michael had painted her.

"We must allow Michael to dictate the pace," she remarked and, noticing Julia's involuntary grimace, she laughed gently. "You have obviously been the victim of my son's gift for being unpleasant! I am sorry, Julia — it seems rather unfair that you should be involved, but I suppose it is inevitable!"

Julia marvelled at the woman's command of such a difficult situation. As a mother Lady Barbara must be deeply hurt by her son's rejection of his home, yet that indefinable quality known as 'breeding' was helping her to cope with disappointment which would have brought lesser mortals to an emotional standstill.

Crossing the room to gaze down over the splendid gardens, Lady Muirisson seemed almost to be speaking to herself.

"We must be patient, I think. We must try to make allowances for Michael. I do believe he is unaware of his power to hurt people, and this is a difficult time for him, coming back to face people who knew him — and loved him — when he was a child. Michael sometimes finds love harder to accept than hatred."

Julia was stunned by her employer's frankness, and moved by her ability to forgive so easily.

"I will try, Lady Muirisson," Julia replied. "I'm sure he is simply in pain from his injury. He was limping rather badly, I'm afraid, and I was insensitive enough to offer help!"

"No, no, my dear girl — you mustn't blame yourself! Michael had problems, long before his accident, which only he can sort out. I do hope he will find himself, learn to accept, now that he is home at last."

Julia could see that Lady Barbara was lost in her own thoughts, and she left the room quietly to return to her duties. Yet even the beauty of the Blue Drawing Room could not hold her attention for long. Her thoughts strayed constantly to Michael and the strange and potent mixture of emotions he had aroused in her.

She went over and over the scene in her mind, thinking of all the things she should have said, how she should have helped in a more subtle way. But still, when she remembered the weight of his body as he leaned on her arm her face would blush pink, not with embarrassment, but with the memory of his touch. Tearing her mind from that moment, she tried to remember how needlessly rude he had been. After all, she pondered, many people lived with pain, day after day, year after year, with none of the comforts Michael had to cushion him against hardship. Yet, so often, these people were filled with the joy of life, inspiring people around them, making more fortunate people feel ashamed of their petty moans and groans.

She was tempted to think that Michael's real problem lay in his immense arrogance. He had been from all accounts, a complete egoist, and anything less than perfection simply did not fit in with his vision of himself! Now, with all the bitterness of his accident festering in him, he had all the makings of a monster — a loathsome figure!

Instinct warned her that Michael spelled danger. She sensed that he would oppose her continued presence here. She was a free thinker, and he demanded subservience. They were perfect enemies and she would surely be best advised to keep her distance.

Dinner that evening, instead of the family celebration which had been planned, was a subdued and stilted affair. Michael was in everyone's thoughts, yet no-one wished to mention his name.

Instead, their conversation focussed on the arrangements for the Dinner and Dance to be held the following evening to publicise and celebrate the opening of the castle to the public. Of the fifty invited guests, several would stay overnight at Berristane, and Julia had been entrusted with the organisation. They talked of floral decorations and where the musical ensemble should be seated; of the allocation of guest rooms, and the booking of taxis to meet the ferry: but their thoughts were elsewhere. Until now the dinner had been looked forward to as a reward for all the hard work and preparation, but Michael's arrival had thrown a shadow over it for everyone.

They were all afraid to voice their real

fears; that Michael would decide to mar the event, either by conspicuous absence, or by attending and behaving badly. He could so easily hurt and upset his family even more, and Julia felt angry on their behalf. She was determined to do everything in her power to prevent him from ruining the evening.

The following morning Julia drove Lady Barbara to the Lodge, before going on to the nearby village on castle business. She could sense that the older woman, although outwardly composed, was nervous of meeting her elder son again.

"Was he very difficult yesterday? And his poor face — Robert says it seems to be healing well." She seemed to hope that Julia could offer her some comfort.

"Well, I have to admit, Lady Muirisson, that he was rather overpowering. But he is still a very fine-looking man. The facial scarring is barely noticeable." She could hardly tell a man's mother than he was still overwhelmingly attractive and that she had been mesmerised by his physical appearance! But Lady Barbara seemed more at ease as they reached the Lodge. The door opened and Michael came to greet his mother, opening his arms to welcome her. Julia was amazed at the warmth of his embrace as he hugged his mother, laughing and kissing her cheek as though he had caused her no upset or concern the previous day. She was even more surprised when turning towards the car, he spoke to her. "Good morning, Miss Markman. How pleasant to see you again! Will you come in for coffee?"

"No . . . no, thank you," stammered Julia, dazzled by his blazing blue eyes, alive with mocking laughter, so unlike the expression which had haunted her through a restless night. "I have some errands to do in the village. I'll collect Lady Muirisson later."

"As you wish! Now, come along Mother! You must advise me on how to get this place into shape." And with a dismissive wave to Julia he drew his delighted mother towards the Lodge.

His welcome had seemed genuine and Julia was pleased for his mother, yet distrust of the great swing in Michael's mood grew in her mind during the morning as she went about, finalising arrangements for the evening's dinner. Which image of Michael was the reality? Was his teasing good humour this morning a truer reflection of his character? Had he simply been exhausted and in pain yesterday?

Whatever the answer, there could be no doubt that his mother was much happier as Julia drove her home. She said little about

43

their reunion, but she glowed with pleasure, and that in itself was enough for Julia.

Michael had also promised to be present for the dinner that evening, much to everyone's relief. Perhaps, as Lady Barbara had said, it was just a matter of making allowances. The afternoon was so hectic, with guests arriving on each ferry, and endless last-minute touches requiring her attention, that Julia had little time to think further about Michael, and it was not until that evening, as she prepared for dinner that she found to her dismay that she had not really forgotten the effect he had had upon her.

She was standing in front of a full-length mirror, arranging her hair and putting the finishing touches to her make-up. Stepping back, she gazed for several minutes at the slim figure reflected there, clad only in flimsy, French lingerie, its peach silk complementing her skin tones. Her face flushed with the sudden realisation that her long self-appraisal was conducted with Michael in mind. As she looked at the image she had been wondering what he would think of her. Worse, the clinging silk jersey dress in deep jade green which lay ready on the bed was the sexiest garment she possessed. Subconsciously she had been dressing as though for a lover!

For a moment she considered selecting another dress, but she was already late and, besides, this was just too adolescent for words! The man disliked her, she disliked him. Didn't she? So what did it matter how she dressed? Drinks were already being served when she joined the company downstairs.

"That," breathed Robert as he fetched a glass of sherry for her, "is what I call a dress!"

"Not too daring?" Julia whispered, a final doubt still remaining.

"Not at all! But you'll make every other woman here look positively dowdy!" He chuckled with such obvious delight that Julia herself stifled a giggle.

Soon she was involved in a heated discussion about the cost of living on the island, a topic near to the hearts of many present, and it was only when the guests were being ushered into the diningroom that she finally caught sight of Michael, leaning nonchalantly against the magnificent Adam fireplace, glass in hand. He was surveying the scene with a mocking smile and, as she caught his eye, he inclined his head towards her, his blue eyes fixed on her face. Like a silly teenager she felt her stomach lurch at the sight of him and she was relieved to find

Robert beckoning her to the diningroom where she soon became involved in yet more earnest discussions, this time about the ferry service's many faults.

The evening was certainly a great success. Amongst the tourist officers, journalists, friends and guests present every comment on the castle seemed to be complimentary. After dinner Julia acted as guide to several groups, showing them round the public apartments and educational displays. She felt a glow of satisfaction that her efforts to show the castle's treasures to best effect seemed to meet with universal approval. As she came downstairs after her third tour of duty, Lady Barbara insisted that she go off and join in the dancing. "You must enjoy yourself, too, after all your hard work." She turned to a group of guests. "I can't tell you how wonderful this young woman is! I don't know how we'd have managed without her."

There was no shortage of partners for Julia, as energetic country dances were followed by quicksteps and dreamy waltzes. As she was moving around the floor she would catch sign of Michael, usually talking to several guests, yet somehow remaining detached and aloof. He did not dance, but that was hardly surprising, in front of so many naturally anxious onlookers.

Finally she decided she must have some fresh air, and slipped quietly through the french windows and onto the little terrace which overlooked the bay.

The sound of the music drifted out over the terrace as Julia swayed in time to its rhythm. It was a mild evening, as yet barely dark, a slight breeze ruffling the trees which screened the terrace from the dancers inside. She was entranced by the beauty of the scene, by the sweet scents of the early summer's evening and perhaps, too, intoxicated by the excitement of the past weeks. Humming gently to herself, she danced alone to the music.

He took her in his arms without a word, fitting his movements so easily to hers. She was only mildly surprised that he had followed her — after all, she realised, hadn't she hoped he would? Here, alone with her, he would be able to dance.

But she was not prepared for the sudden and overwhelming response of her body to his as they moved across the terrace. She burned for him, offering no resistance as he held her so closely that she felt sure he must feel the heat of her body pour over him. Lifting her face towards his for the first time, she caught her breath in admiration and, responding to some inner demand, gently lifted her hand to caress the line of the scar with her fingertips. It was as though an electric current passed between them. Catching her still closer to him, he crushed his lips against hers and her mouth opened to him with a surge of desire which overwhelmed. Her fingers moved to the nape of his neck, threading through the tendrils which curled there. She was lost to herself, her body merging into his.

Abruptly, he pulled away from her, almost pushing her aside.

"Michael . . . !" she gasped.

"Well! That was what you planned, wasn't it?" he spat out. "It was your intention! Or are you dressed like that to thrill old Menteith?"

Tears of shock and embarrassment filled her eyes as she turned away. My god, what have I done? She thought wildly. Why is he so angry?

"No doubt you are skilled in manipulating men, Miss Markman, and I'll admit you were made for seduction, but your wiles are wasted on me, because I know your game!"

Unable to face any more, she ran from the terrace, horrified that a dream should so suddenly turn nightmare! She felt betrayed by her own body and devastated by Michael's cruel pretence of passion!

THREE

She was already awake when Jenny came in with her teatray the next morning. Despite the sunlight streaming through the chintzy curtains, Julia felt no desire to face the day. Her head ached with the weeping which had finally lulled her into a fitful sleep. She was thankful that she would have the day to herself. Somehow she had to put yesterday behind her and get back on an even keel before the 'Grand Opening of the Castle and Grounds' tomorrow. There was so much to be done!

Jenny seemed to be lingering, and when Julia caught sight of the single scarlet rose on her tray, she assumed that the girl had added this special touch.

"Jenny! How lovely — and how thoughtful . . ."

"There's a note with it, Miss. Under the plate. Lord Michael was in the kitchen 'fore seven this morning, making sure they were on your tray. He made me swear you'd get them!" The girl giggled nervously and bustled from the room.

"Well!" thought Julia. She turned the fragile stem in her fingers, noticing that the thorns had been carefully removed. The bloom was perfect, its petals delicate, and still tightly folded, their edges tinged with the faintest purple. She lifted the envelope and gazed at it. Barely recovered from the previous evening, for which she blamed herself, she felt unable to cope with more from Michael. Now, she simply wanted to keep her distance from him, forget whatever brainstorm, or childish infatuation, had overthrown her common sense. But she could not leave the letter unopened.

She read the lines very slowly, determined not to be upset by anything he might have to say. *Dear Miss Markman,* she read. *I am so sorry! Please forgive my ludicrous behaviour. The incident will not be repeated.*

I would be most grateful if you would meet me in the Main Hall at 10 a.m. to discuss some administrative duties and see your work in the apartments.

What a peculiar apology this was, mused Julia. A humble plea for forgiveness, a single red rose and a business appointment, all thrown together in the most disconcerting way! Nevertheless, even on a 'day off' she could hardly refuse his request — or was it a command? — to show him around.

She dressed quickly, deciding that a sweat-shirt, jeans and sneakers were sufficiently nondescript and brushing her hair back severely into a ponytail. Her face was scrubbed and fresh, and just a touch of eye make-up concealed any remaining traces of her tears. Seductive she certainly would not be!

He was already in the hall when she arrived. Like her, he had dressed casually — although Julia was sure the sweater was pure cashmere, and he looked so different from her smooth, dinner-suited tormentor of the previous evening.

He obviously intended to make no reference either to his behaviour, or to his apology and she was grateful for the business-like attitude he adopted. He asked her several questions about the administration of staff duties during castle opening times, and the security arrangements which had been made. He appeared satisfied with her intelligent answers and command of the situation, and soon suggested that they go upstairs, "to see your skills in practice!"

He seemed to find the stairs difficult and Julia, although avoiding his eyes, sensed that he was steeling himself against pain. On the landing he stopped. Julia assumed first that he wanted to rest but he was looking up at his portrait as though seeing it for the first time. Eventually he spoke, his voice tight with bitterness. "Rather out-of-date, wouldn't you say, Miss Markman? A picture from the past, like all the others?" He was daring her to answer, taunting her with an impossible question.

"I think it's an excellent likeness, Sir. But I would be happier if you would call me Julia." She turned to climb the stairs, avoiding his gaze. How could she tell him that the portrait cast only a shadow of his fabulously handsome face? The scar which made him even more attractive, also made him blind to his own powers.

"Well then," he replied, "I think you had better call me Michael, since it appears that you are a part of the family now." Julia felt that she could hear a trace of irony in his voice, but she ignored it and continued up the stairs.

Once upstairs he seemed more relaxed, and Julia was surprised at his obviously genuine appreciation of her work. He moved around the public rooms, pausing here and there to view the effect from a particular angle, and complimenting her on her 'eye' for design and detail. She watched, fascinated, as he lifted and examined some of the precious silver and china displayed on the magnificent polished sideboards. He loved these beautiful objects, she mused, almost surprised at the discovery. Yet he had been born and raised here; why should she have expected his recent history, as a shallow jet-setter, to change a carefully-nurtured love of beautiful things?

He asked after several particular pieces of porcelain, including the figure Julia had so admired of the white-gowned girl. She showed him the dresser in the 'Duchess Louise Bedroom', where she had placed the figure. "I love this piece," he said quietly, almost to himself. Held in his large, tanned hands, with all their obvious power, the white-gowned girl seemed even more fragile, as though he might, at any moment, crush her to powder. But instead, he cradled her in his palm, caressing the fine folds of the gown with his finger-tips. A shiver ran down Julia's spine.

"Perfection. Absolute perfection," Michael said. "It's the detail! Look at her tiny fingers — the features of the face." He brought the figure to her, so that she could share his delight in it. "Don't be afraid to touch it," he said and then, looking straight at her, he murmured, "Your fingers are very gentle. They couldn't do her any harm." Julia knew that he was referring to her spontaneous gesture of the previous evening. She tried to think of something to say, but at that moment he moved away, launching into a summary of the place in history occupied by 'Duchess Louise'.

"Quite a lady!" he laughed. "She was before her time. A woman of truly independent mind and great beauty. Usually a terrifying combination!" They continued their tour of the rooms with no further revelations of his complex character, and if Julia's thoughts were persistently interrupted by the memory of the delicate figurine in his unthreatening yet all-powerful hands, she managed to conceal from him her lack of concentration.

He was talkative, asking searching and often abrupt questions about the work which had been done in the past few weeks, suggesting minor alterations, new ideas which might be introduced later.

Julia was surprised by his interest in the castle. The impression of him given by Robert had led her to expect Michael to be at best, indifferent, at worst, totally hostile to the whole project. Although he now held the title, he had shown so little interest in his domain before. Perhaps, she pondered, he was determined to become involved if he could not continue with his former lifestyle.

Shortly before lunch Julia drove him back to the Lodge. She was relieved that the morning had passed without incident. It might be possible for her to grow to like him eventually, if she could put the previous evening behind her.

He made no attempt to hold her back, simply wishing her luck for the forthcoming week. "You'll be very busy, I should think; as, indeed, I will be myself — endless numbers of tradesmen are due to make this place habitable!" It was as though he were dismissing her.

Over lunch Robert was in an inquisitive mood. He pestered her with questions about his brother. Julia felt that he was trying to assess her reaction to this charismatic figure, to find out whether his warning to her had been in vain. But, fond though she was of Robert, she did not feel inclined to air her confusion to him. She had, in the space of a couple of days, experienced many emotions, so violently extreme, that it seemed impossible that they were responses to one man. Her answers to Robert's questions were brief and evasive, and she excused herself early, saying that she must make a final check on the souvenir stock of the castle shop.

The staff she met as she went round the castle that afternoon seemed as excited about the following day as she was herself. In the main rooms, the guides read and re-read their notes on the various items visitors might wish to ask about, and swotted the background material about the castle's fascinating past. The ladies in the tearoom marvelled at the benefits of the coffee-maker and microwave, but bemoaned the use of gingham table covers.

"Sure to be spills! Sure to be! There'll be a terrible lot of washing!" they agreed. Julia smiled sympathetically, but assured them that the local laundrette, often under-used by the permanent island population, was delighted at the prospect of dirty linen!

The opening of the castle as a tourist attraction had been enthusiastically received by the locals. Many of them relied on their summer work to keep them throughout the year, and anything which encouraged visitors was fine by them. Besides, the castle was now employing many more staff, some of them young men and women who had previously been unemployed. No wonder the excitement spread beyond the castle walls!

As she ironed out minor problems, re-assured staff, answered phonecalls, and made last-minute checks with press photographers and reporters who had agreed to cover the opening, Julia discovered the pleasure of knowing she had command of the situation, and was doing her job coolly and efficiently. In a short time she had made herself, if not indispensable, at least very important to the smooth running of the castle. Perhaps one day in the distant future there would be other things in her life more vital but, for now her work, and the satisfaction it gave her, was the focus of her energy.

Dinner that evening was a quiet affair, with only one guest; the Tourist Board chairwoman who would open the castle to the public by acting as its first 'paying' visitor. The atmosphere was relaxed: the hard work was over for the moment, and everything possible had been done to ensure success.

After the meal Julia and Robert sat outside on the terrace, chatting in the gathering dusk, that magical time known in Scotland as the gloaming. Robert had become a firm friend and Julia felt at ease with him. This evening he made no attempt to discuss his brother and, perhaps because of that, Julia found herself mentioning Michael, casually remarking on his enthusiasm for the castle's treasures. "It surprised me, somehow," she explained. "It seemed so strange, watching him touch that beautiful porcelain with such reverence, such love."

"Out of character, you mean?" smiled Robert.

"Well — I'm hardly in a position to judge what his real character is, am I? I hardly know him." Julia thought of Robert's ominous warnings about Michael. Had they all been affected by the high emotions of his return home, their sympathy for his physical pain? Perhaps it was all a storm in a teacup.

"Perhaps you haven't known him long," Robert admitted, "but he seems to be impressed by you, and if Michael actually likes you, you may get the opportunity of finding out what makes him tick. I'm his brother, but I couldn't really say I know him!" There was regret in his voice as he spoke these final words and, as darkness fell, the two sat on in silence, wrapped in their private thoughts of Michael.

In the days which followed, however, there was little time for thoughts of anything except work. Each night Julia fell into bed too exhausted to think, after a day of endless activity. She loved every minute of it;

the visitors' questions and problems, their lost children and cameras, their enthusiasm and admiration for the castle. The staff, too, quickly recognised her ability to cope with impending disasters such as the failure of the local bakery to deliver the required number of doughnuts, and the insistence by the less-charming visitors, that no flower bed or seeded area, however marked, was sacred!

Julia discovered a tact and diplomacy she had not known she possessed, and considered everything an exciting challenge, but still, it was undeniably exhausting.

At the end of the second week Lady Barbara sought her out and insisted that she take time off. "I'll hear no excuses, young woman! I should tell you, my motives are entirely selfish — I simply don't want you to work yourself into a state of collapse, and need weeks off. Go on, enjoy a break. You deserve it." Julia could hardly refuse. The castle was busy, but any teething troubles had been dealt with, and even she was not indispensable.

"In any case," added Lady Barbara, vainly trying to sound casual, "I think Michael needs your assistance. Could you pop down to the Lodge and see him, dear?"

It was a fine evening and Julia, relaxed

after her shower and change, and pleased at the prospect of a few days off, decided to walk down to the Lodge. She had not spent any time alone in Michael's company since the castle opening, exchanging only brief greetings when she saw him, and avoiding him on the rare occasions when he dined with the family.

Her confusion over the first encounters had faded, but still she felt nervous at the thought of being required to 'assist' him.

When she arrived at the Lodge he was sitting outside, reading. But her attention was immediately focussed on a silver grey Mercedes convertible, its soft top removed, which stood in the driveway.

"What a gorgeous car!" she exclaimed, forgetting any nervousness.

"Think you could drive her?" Michael asked and, as she laughed in reply, "No — I'm serious! That's the assistance I asked for, you see. It's just been delivered, and my leg isn't up to driving any distance yet. Not in comfort anyway. So I thought, if you hadn't seen the island, I could let you drive me round tomorrow."

Julia was taken aback. He seemed so happy, like a child with a new toy. And he had mentioned his injury almost casually. Against her conscious efforts to remain aloof she felt a flood of affection for him. What must it cost him, a professional driver, a very virile and athletic man, to be reduced to admitting he needed her to drive him? She stifled any hint of pity, recognising how dangerous a sentiment it could be.

She responded freely to his childlike pleasure and when he grasped her hand to invite her indoors, it seemed the most natural thing in the world.

"Come and admire my new decor! Do you think it qualifies as a *Vogue* interior?" The Lodge had been transformed. The huge ingle, lit by a log fire, still dominated the central room and everything else had been arranged to suit it. Two beautiful burgundy leather couches faced each other in front of the fireplace, the floor between them covered by a delicately woven rug. Small tables carried heavy stone lamps, obviously designed to cast a soft and flattering light as evening approached.

On the side walls, bookcases were crammed, somewhat haphazardly, with books — leather-bound, paperbacked — all there for reading and not for decoration.

"Do you approve?" he asked, and it seemed as though it mattered to him that she should.

"It really is beautiful. It's so warm, so

welcoming." Julia loved the room.

"I'll venture into the kitchen and fix us some supper — it's still being refitted. But have a look at the bedroom — if you dare!"

Julia smiled at his flirtatious teasing. He was a changed man, and she liked it.

His bedroom was, undeniably, a man's room. There were no pastel shades or flowered prints here. The furniture, including a huge mirrored wardrobe, was plain and white, but everything else was a sensual mixture of textures and shades. The bed, a huge king-size, was covered by a screen-printed silk covering in deep blue, patterned with touches of jade. The carpet, with its thick luxurious pile, was perfectly matched in the velvet curtains. And if the livingroom had been a public room, this room was for him. Everywhere lay his personal possessions, books, magazines, photographs; a television, video recorder and hi-fi were grouped to one side of the bed. And over everything, the fragrance of the expensive cologne he had been wearing that evening on the terrace. Julia hugged her arms tightly to her sides as she tried to quell the tide of feeling which flowed through her, but she recognised with some consternation that her response to the room was one of physical desire. She longed to be in his arms again, feel the strength and firmness of his body against hers.

"As you can see, this is my hiding-place." His voice, so close to her, startled Julia from the embarrassing intimacy of her thoughts. She prayed that he could not read her mind!

"It's very nice . . ." she stammered.

"But perhaps not to your taste?" he asked quizzically, as though amused by her obvious discomfiture. "Or too much like a spider's web on the lookout for careless flies!" If he was mocking her, it was without cruelty and soon, over supper, Julia regained some composure.

She enjoyed Michael's company, finding it easy to talk to him. With the skill of one relaxed in female company, he prompted her into telling him a great deal about her adult life, particularly her time in France.

"And does Berristane live up to your expectations?" he asked.

"I don't know what I expected!" Julia replied frankly. "But I love it here. To be paid to do something you would happily do for nothing . . . ! What more could anyone ask?"

There was silence in the room and Julia slowly noticed that Michael, who had been listening so attentively to her, was lost in thought. He sat, hunched forward on the couch in front of her, his gaze fixed on the glowing fire. Instinctively she understood the line of his thoughts.

"I loved my job too." His voice was taut with control when he finally spoke. "I know you probably don't consider motor racing a 'job', but it was my whole life.

"Everyone thinks it's so glamorous. The champagne, the speed, the laurel wreath, the girls, the money! They don't see the hard slog behind the scenes, especially in a small independent team like ours. Nights on end when you don't see a bedroom. And if you did, all you would want was to sleep — alone!" He smiled wryly, remembering.

"But you must have made some money from it?" Julia asked, ignoring his final remarks.

"Oh, yes. But not what other people imagine!" He looked directly at her. "Do you really think I'd have had Berristane turned into a circus if I'd had the money to do otherwise?"

"But Michael, you're wrong! It's not like that!" Julia was defensive on a subject close to her heart. "It really isn't the intrusion into your family's life that you might expect. And the visitors are mostly decent people, delighted to be allowed the chance to see such beautiful things. You just don't see much of what's going on; you've been so busy down here."

He smiled at her, touched by her willingness to rally to the cause, even if it meant disagreeing with him.

"More coffee?" he asked.

"No, thank you. I really must get back."

Julia wanted to end the evening on this relaxed note. She sensed that her willingness to assert herself might lead her into clashes with Michael in the future. She did not want to start now.

She was to drive the Mercedes back to the castle and garage it overnight. A picnic basket would be prepared for them, and she was to pick Michael up at the Lodge at ten the next morning.

"Drive carefully!" he said, as she strapped herself in and examined the dashboard, and controls. "And I don't mean just because of the car," he added and, to her absolute amazement, he bent forward and kissed her lightly on the cheek. Her face flushed scarlet, but she willed herself to concentrate on the car. Only when she had left it safe in the garage did she allow her fingertips to touch her cheek, as though asking whether his kiss had been real.

How silly, she thought. It was a habit in this family, a simple gesture of friendship, not a sign of sudden and passionate attachment. Robert and his mother always embraced on meeting or leaving one another. Indeed, when she thought about it, Robert had recently kissed her cheek on bidding her goodnight. It was nothing, she reasoned, just an alternative to hand-shaking! Heavens, think of the French!

But for her, it was not so. She burned with the memory of Michael's lips, the light caress with which he had stirred her that evening, and the cruel mockery of his embrace the night on the terrace.

She had been attracted to a man before, but she could not recall this frightening sensation of being set aflame by the mere touch of a hand. And always, she had had the ability to back away from men she knew were wrong for her. What of Michael? Was he simply trying to ridicule her? He was a man of the world and he must be able to read her attraction to him in her eyes. Why did he want to bewilder her with a series of physical 'messages' which contradicted each other?

She was so agitated that she knew she could not sleep, and decided instead to write to her cousin Anne. Although she had meant to stick to safe ground she found herself writing about Michael.

The playboy prodigal son, has, of course returned home! No doubt the gossip columns will sorely miss him! I find him a very difficult man to understand. I suppose we must make allowances for his behaviour while he is still recovering.

Sometimes I think he dislikes me. But at others — well, as you can see, Anne, he is at least interesting!

She hoped that her words sounded objective. Anne was notorious for reading correctly between the lines. Julia smiled at the thought of her London 'family'. She did miss them, although she loved Rosa. Lifting her pen again, she begged them to think of spending a few days here when their holiday time arrived.

Writing the letter, renewing her bond with people who loved and cared for her, made Julia feel more secure, less vulnerable to the strangeness of her new relationship with Michael and soon she felt ready to go to bed. As she drifted off to sleep, she wondered again what tomorrow would bring. Which side of Michael would be on show?

FOUR

The morning was beautiful as she drew up outside the Lodge and sounded the horn. Michael appeared almost immediately and Julia noticed with some apprehension that he seemed to be limping more heavily than before. Perhaps it was worse for him in the morning, she guessed, but she said nothing, simply giving herself over to the enjoyment of his company, the beauty of the island and the thrill of driving this wonderful car.

The scenery through which they passed was indeed breathtaking. Every few miles Michael would tell her to draw into the side of the road so that they could absorb the beauty which surrounded them.

What surprised Julia most was the variety of landscape. Around the castle, woodland and farm grazing land dominated the wide sweep of the bay yet, as they drove north, they seemed to enter a new kingdom of jagged peaks and huge rock-falls. The sun glinted on the slate surfaces of high mountains, turning them silver. Each bend in the road revealed a new perspective, of forest, moorland or valley.

Finally the road began to dip downhill, towards the sea again, and glimpses of a tiny village, its cottages scattered haphazardly along the narrow ribbon of the shore road. Michael indicated a turning where Julia should stop and when they got out of the car, she discovered that the sandy path ahead led, in a matter of yards, to a pebble beach so quiet and private that they seemed to be the only people in the world to have discovered its existence. Together they fetched the picnic hamper and spread a rug in the shelter of one of the low sandy hillocks which hid the beach from the road.

"This must be your first experience of a Muirisson picnic!" Michael laughed at Julia's wide-eyed reaction to the overflowing hamper.

"Well — it certainly hasn't much in common with egg sandwiches and ginger-beer at Brighton," she agreed, as Michael revealed chicken, cold ham, salmon, vegetable salad, gateaux, and endless other delights.

"And not forgetting the Chablis," he said, flourishing an impressive-looking wine bottle. "Don't worry, a little of this won't threaten your driving. Do you know much about wine?"

Despite her time in France, Julia still knew little on the subject, but she was aware that the greeny gold wine Michael was pouring was certainly not a supermarket brand.

"All you need to know," said Michael, "is whether or not you like it. Forget all the affectation which surrounds the whole business of wine."

It was a magically beautiful day. The sky's blue brilliance was veiled here and there with the merest wisps of cloud. Julia marvelled at the clarity of the air, free from the tiniest hint of smoke or dust. As they ate and drank, Michael talked at great length about the island, about its history, its unique geology, its inexplicable ability to capture the hearts and minds of those who came to visit.

"You would be amazed at the number of people who come for a summer holiday, and end up coming to live here permanently! Sometimes they have to change their whole lifestyle, but they seem spell-bound by the place."

"How could you bear to be away for so long?" Julia asked.

"Well, I suppose it was partly the tendency many youngsters have, to reject 'home' almost on principle. But then, while my father was alive, visits were pure hell anyway. He didn't approve of my choice of career, you see, and when I did come home there were always remarks about 'playboys', 'rich lay-abouts', 'dropouts'. In the end it wasn't worth it, but sometimes I ached just to be here." He paused, lying back on the rug and looking up into the clear sky. "You are a remarkably crafty young woman, you know! I very rarely talk so much about myself."

"Is it so difficult?" Julia smiled, intrigued that a man as egotistical as Michael was supposed to be should be loath to talk about himself.

"Not so much difficult, as dangerous. Come on — can you skim stones?" He had closed the door on himself and the moment of insight was over.

As she followed him across the giant pebbles, Julia wondered at the complexity of the man who now stood at the water's edge, throwing stones to create ever-widening circles, skimming stones which bounced across the gentle waves like live things. She had expected him to be shallow and arrogant, and her early meetings with him had seemed to confirm this. But last night, and again now, she was seeing a different man; an entrancing combination of strength, self-assurance and vulnerability . . . a combination of qualities designed to melt the heart of any woman.

She must have been staring at him without realising it for suddenly Michael was looking at her, his eyes searching her face, as though seeking an answer for some question he could not bring himself to ask. Julia's heart leaped as she met his gaze. He moved nearer and took her gently in his arms, enfolding, sheltering her as he lowered his head to hers.

That night on the terrace he had burned her with his touch, had made her afraid of him and of herself. Now, alone with him on this wild and beautiful shore, Julia was not afraid. He was so powerful, yet his touch was gentle, his hands flowed over her body like a spell, holding her to him, locked against the strength and firmness of him. She felt no threat, only a strange sense of belonging.

At last he released her, raising his hand to caress her blushing cheek. "I am glad you have forgiven me," he said, his voice low and gruff with emotion. "I treated you badly — I'm sorry." He pulled her to him again, allowing her head to rest on his chest, and they stood there for some time befor he led her slowly back towards the dunes. They tidied the hamper, and returned to the car in silence as though both were unsure of what had passed between them on the beach. As Julia prepared to set off, Michael touched her hand as it lay on the steering wheel.

"Julia, I don't know what that meant; what happened just now." He seemed to be searching for some way of explaining.

"You don't need to explain anything . . ." Julia began.

"No, no, perhaps not. But I need to understand. Things are so difficult for me just now. It . . . Sometimes I don't act consistently. I . . ." His voice tailed off into silence and Julia started the engine. Best not to give too much significance to Michael's kisses, or to his explanations, she thought, trying hard to convince herself. But her body still glowed with the memory of his touch.

He remained silent for several miles, lost in thought once more, but Julia was content to drive, closing out any thoughts about his behaviour. Gradually he became communicative again, turning himself into a tour guide for her benefit, pointing out anything of particular interest or beauty. The relaxed and happy atmosphere was restored as they drove south again along the island's western shore. Here the scenery grew more wild and the cottages more sparsely scattered. The tide which washed the huge boulders on the shoreline was an ocean tide, powerful and unrelenting.

"This is my favourite part of the island," Michael said. "This and Glen Mhor. I love the wildness of it. You come here and all your problems shrink into a reasonable perspective."

Julia told him of a conversation she had had with a visitor the previous day. The old man had spent every holiday on Rosa for forty years.

"It's a magical place," the old man had told her. "Places like Scarborough, or Blackpool — they're great for entertainment and shows. But Rosa! Well — Rosa's good for your soul!"

It was late afternoon when they drew up outside the Lodge. Julia could not remember when she had last enjoyed such a day and she told Michael so.

"Me too," he replied but his voice seemed troubled. Taking her hand to kiss it lightly he spoke so quietly that she could barely hear. "But promise me — on the shore; don't — try not to make anything of that which wasn't there!" Julia looked at him, bewildered, yet understanding that he was trying to protect her in some way. She smiled at him, trying to appear untroubled.

As she walked up to the castle alone she decided once and for all, that any relationship she had with Michael would be unlike anything she had known before. He was a complex man and, she feared, dangerous. But what she felt for him was equally complex. She must simply take each day as it came.

She woke late the following morning, having slept soundly after her day in the island's strong sea air. After breakfast she browsed through the private library before joining Lady Barbara, who had invited Julia to join her on a walk round the castle grounds. Julia suspected that her employer had an ulterior motive and was not surprised when Michael's name was raised.

"Do you think he enjoyed your day out yesterday?" she asked. "How did he seem?"

Julia hoped that her expression would not reflect her thoughts at the mention of Michael's name. "Most of the time he seemed quite happy, quite relaxed in fact," she reassured. "He was fun to be with until . . ." She blushed. "It's hard to explain Lady Barbara. It was almost as though he felt threatened by his happiness. He was really quite withdrawn later. Perhaps I bored him . . ."

she finished lamely.

Lady Barbara smiled. "I hardly think so, my dear. It is quite clear to me that Michael finds you attractive. But perhaps he has not given you quite the same impression?"

Julia was touched by the older woman's gentleness. She was not prying, but she cared deeply for her son and it was natural that she should want him to be happy and untroubled. Julia felt it easy to confide in her.

"I simply don't know what he thinks of me — if he thinks anything," she sighed.

"And that upsets you? You have grown fond of him, haven't you?"

"He is an immensely attractive man, Lady Barbara, but he seems to swing between complete self-assurance and . . ."

Lady Barbara nodded in agreement. "You seem to understand him rather well, Julia. He is very confused, and it worries me greatly. Please be patient with him. He is still in some pain, and it must be hard for him."

They strolled on through the beautiful gardens, coming now into full-summer splendour. They talked of Michael's accident, of his rejection of family help or company in its aftermath.

"Sometimes, I think he needs jolting out

of this depression," Lady Barbara said. "I know he loathes being less than fit, and the facial scarring seems to worry him a great deal."

"But his face . . ." Julia hesitated in embarrassment, but her companion turned to her questioningly. "Michael's face is wonderful. He is the most attractive man I have ever seen." How odd to make such remarks to a man's mother.

"Oh, it's hard for me to be objective, Julia. But he was such a beautiful child, quite striking in fact. Unfortunately, he was aware far too early of the power of his appearance. He could be angelic, charming, and then behave appallingly the next moment. Everyone assumed he was so self-confident, so self-assured. But, I'm sure he was afraid much of the time."

Julia was moved by the older woman's frankness, her obvious love for her child.

"Afraid?" she asked.

"I think he's always been afraid that people claimed to love him for his appearance, or his status, or his money. He could never trust their love, and so he refused to show love in return."

The two women sat together, looking out over the bay, their conversation drifting to other, more mundane topics, though their thoughts remained with Michael. At last Lady Barabra made to return to the castle, but Julia decided to walk on towards the Lodge. There was no reason why she should not call on Michael, to thank him for his guided tour.

There was no answer to her knock, but the door stood wide open and Julia went in. She called his name, but there was no reply. He could not be far away. Should she wait for him, or look outside? As she hesitated, he walked in.

"Hello, Michael!" she cried. "I thought I'd . . ." His expression silenced her.

"Do you usually enter someone's home in his absence?" he snapped.

"I'm sorry." Julia was caught unawares by the sharpness of his manner. "I didn't think you'd have gone far so —"

"No! Oh no — the cripple can only have hobbled a few steps! Was that your idea?"

"Michael!" Julia's anger at his ridiculous rudeness banished her embarrassment. "I came to thank you for yesterday, actually."

"And you think that what happened yesterday entitles you to waltz in here as though you owned it? I came here for privacy!"

"You should take more care to close your front door then!" Julia shouted back, furi-

78

ous now. How dare he behave like this, like a spoiled and arrogant child! "Go on, lock yourself away like a hermit!"

"I will — I will," he replied through clenched teeth. "And you will not come here to spy on me!"

"Spy? You flatter yourself, my lord! It's time you removed the chip from your shoulder and tried being grateful!"

"Grateful? For this?" The anguish in his voice as he thumped his fist against his injured thigh tempted Julia to stop, but her anger was still too great.

"At least you're alive!" she gasped. "You'll get better, and your vanity will recover. My parents were killed outright in their car crash. A drunk driver robbed them of any chance even to fight for life. They never had the option of moping and whining as you do, punishing other people for your pain!"

"Get out!" he yelled, but she had already turned on her heel and run from the Lodge, tears of rage and pain streaming down her face. She hated him! How dare he treat her like this? How dare he!

On and on she walked, leaving the estate at its boundary and following the track towards the farms which bordered it.

Gradually she became calmer and with her renewed composure came regret that she had ventured near the Lodge at all. Perhaps there was a grain of truth in Michael's accusations. Perhaps, despite his attempts to warn her off, she had assumed the beginnings of a relationship with him. Hadn't she gone to the Lodge in the hope of another sign that he was attracted to her?

Slowly she became more aware of the countryside through which she was walking. She slowed her pace from the furious strides with which she had begun her retreat from Michael, and looked about her.

Highland cattle, like four-legged hippies, grazed in the field by the track. They watched her slow progress with glowering curiosity. She recognised a small herd of elegant Charolais cattle, a new investment for a group of local farmers. Julia giggled, wondering if they were snooty and superior with the more familiar Ayrshire and Galloway herd.

The weather was perfect as it had been the previous day, and Julia wandered on, losing track of the time until she began to feel pangs of hunger, and realised that it must be long past lunch-time. Regretfully she turned back, and had walked a mile or so when she heard the noise of a motor engine behind and the Range Rover crunched to a halt beside her.

"Want a lift?" Robert asked and Julia, growing hungrier every minute, readily agreed.

She said nothing of her quarrel with Michael, chatting instead about the things she had noticed on her walk. Robert was full of conversation about the problems of financing the new farm machinery required on the tenant farms he had been visiting.

"You really enjoy the life here, don't you?" Julia asked him.

Robert agreed. "I'm not really the Lord-of-the-Manor type. I'd rather be a farmer! If I thought Michael would stay on here permanently, take responsibility for the castle and grounds, I could let myself get more involved."

Julia looked fixedly out of the window as she steadied her voice. "Don't you think he will stay, then?" She prayed that this sounded like a casual enquiry.

"Oh, I don't know. Who knows what Michael is thinking? I can't see him managing to resist the pull of the jet-set life for much longer!" He laughed. "After all, when your first choice is wine, women, song and fast cars — not necessarily in that order — where does Rosa fit into the picture?"

Julia did not reply. Robert was right, of course. It had been too convenient to forget that Michael's lifestyle until his accident had been light-years from his 'privacy' at the Lodge. The gossip columnists had always been able to gain column inches from his wild exploits on racetracks, in casinos, or in the welcoming arms of some of the world's most glamorous women.

"And talking of big brother . . ." Robert's voice interrupted her wistful thoughts, and to her horror Julia saw that Robert was turning down towards the Lodge. "Won't be a moment," he said. "I've just got to get his signature on some papers. Do you want to come in?"

Julia quickly replied that it wasn't worth it for such a brief time and, indeed, it was only minutes later that Robert emerged with Michael behind him. She swallowed the lump in her throat as he looked in at the driver's window.

"Good afternoon, Julia." He spoke with icy politeness.

"Good afternoon." Robert started the engine, exchanging a final word with his brother before driving off.

"Pardon my saying so," he prompted. "But weren't things a bit chilly back there?"

Julia bit her lip. "We are not on the best of terms at the moment."

"But yesterday . . . Hey! He didn't try

anything on yesterday, did he?" Robert sounded quite perturbed.

"No, not in the way you mean," Julia replied wearily. She knew that Robert meant well, but she was too wretched herself to be able to discuss it with anyone else. "We just quarrelled this morning. I virtually told him to stop feeling sorry for himself."

"Good for you, girl!" Robert exclaimed. "That's what he needs! Don't upset yourself about it." He paused, glancing at her ashen face. Suddenly he spoke with absolute conviction. "You're in love with him."

"Oh, Robert . . ." Julia turned away.

"OK, OK, I shouldn't pry!" He drew to a halt outside the main castle entrance. "But Julia, it's written all over your face." Robert placed a finger under her chin, tilting her face towards him. He smiled with such kindness that her eyes filled with tears. "Oh, my lovely lady — I warned you! Please, please don't get yourself hurt."

"Too late, Robert, too late." Julia smiled wryly, quickly kissing his cheek before climbing out of the Range Rover and waving him off. He was a good friend, and it mattered to her that he cared.

In her room she showered and enjoyed the afternoon tea Jenny had brought to her. Asking that dinner be served here too, Julia decided to stay in her room for the rest of the day, restoring some sense to her jumbled emotions. She decided that she must get back to work tomorrow, immerse herself in activity so that she could avoid Michael. What was all this fuss about? Why should she, who had always been in control of herself, allow any man to treat her so badly?

And yet, how could she forget those moments in his arms, the physical desire which had ruled her then? How could she be cool and distant, protect herself from hurt, when all she wanted was to hold him?

She spent the time that evening reading and listening to the radio and she was writing a letter to Anne when there was a tap at the door. Expecting Jenny to appear with her tray, she was startled when the 'maid' turned out to be Michael.

"What do you want?" she demanded defensively.

"I've brought dinner," he said meekly. "I wanted to talk to you."

"Oh, no! No more talk, Michael, please!" She leaped up, taking the tray from his hands and placing it on the table to cover her letter, which contained his name.

Still, he stood there.

"Look, I've got letters to write, and I'm very tired."

"This is more important than letters," he insisted. "I'm leaving tomorrow."

"Leaving?" At one fell swoop Julia's decision to remain aloof was cast aside.

"Just for a week or so. I'm going to see my specialist, visit some friends. You were right this morning, Julia. I've got to pull myself together."

"Oh, Michael, I didn't mean to be so rude."

"No, you were simply being honest. I know that now. I have to do something to speed my recovery. I'm no use to anyone like this — a wreck."

He sat down in the huge armchair, his head hung low. He was dejected, utterly drained by the emotional turmoil which their quarrel had forced into the open. Julia knelt before him, ready to comfort, to reassure. With a sigh which seemed to be drawn from his innermost self he drew her to him and they were back once more on the windswept shore, locked in a trance of mutual desire.

She rested her head on his chest, hearing the beating of his heart, hypnotised by the thrill of his touch.

His voice when he spoke was quiet, unsteady. "I have to go away. Don't you see, I need to be apart from you?" He stroked her hair. "I don't want to be involved, Julia. It isn't for me, and Rosa isn't for me either, not yet. And I don't want to hurt you." She made to protest, but he silenced her, his finger to her lips. "Physical attraction is one thing, Julia, and I do want you. But you deserve more than that, and I can't give it! You need a man to love and cherish you. Protect you."

"Then why come here, now?" Julia asked, bewildered. "Why not just go without explanation?" She knew even as she spoke that he could not answer her question. He was going because he was afraid, and she could not keep him.

"My life is in London, New York, wherever the excitement is." He went on, almost as though trying to convince himself. "My friends are there. It's where I belong."

He stood up and made for the door.

"Robert's taking me to the early ferry tomorrow. I'll leave these." He placed a set of keys on the table. "Will you look in at the Lodge for me — the workmen are still finishing the kitchen? And drive the car whenever you want, won't you?"

"But if it's only for a week?"

"Well — it may be a little longer. I'll just have to wait and see what the specialist says.

Goodbye Julia. Take care!" And he was gone.

I will not weep, she thought. I will not, I will not. Why cry over something that doesn't even exist? And yet there was the other voice inside her head, telling her that if he was afraid enough to cut himself off from her, there must be hope that he felt more for her than the physical attraction to which he would admit.

"Oh, Michael," she whispered to herself. "Come back to me!" And in that moment she knew that he was the only man in the world for her.

FIVE

It was not difficult for Julia to drown herself in work in the days which followed Michael's departure. Visitors continued to flock to the castle; minor problems of staffing and catering needed her attention; interviews were arranged with Lady Barbara for several London-based glossy magazines. It was absorbing work, presenting new challenges every day. The season was under way now, and there was some discussion of monitoring the number of visitors so as to predict a suitable date for ending their first summer opening.

Although Julia was perfectly well aware that such forward planning was essential, the mention of the season's end chilled her. What would the autumn bring? Would she be asked to stay on? Would she wish to?

They were sitting at breakfast one morning, a week after Michael's departure, when Robert let out a barely suppressed guffaw.

"Well, I'll hand it to him! It doesn't take our boy long to get himself back on the gossip pages! He quoted from the famous columnist and friend of the famous.

"Spotted at the opening of 'Bangels' the city's newest trendy nightspot: former race ace Lord Muirisson (35) and sizzling starlet, Kerrin O'Brienn. Lord Michael, seriously injured in a car crash some months ago, seems, this week, to have re-entered the social whirl, fully recovered, no doubt under the caring eye of the enchanting Miss O'Brienn."

Robert seemed greatly amused by the piece, but, for Julia, the gentle smile she contrived was a triumph over her feelings. She said nothing but, left alone to finish breakfast, she lifted the paper and gazed at the photograph. It was in typical gossip page style. Michael, dashingly handsome in dinner suit and ruffled shirt, stood with a champagne glass in one hand, his other arm draped around the shoulders of a very pretty girl who was gazing longingly up at him.

Why was it that the kind of story she had always dismissed as inventive trivia, not worth reading, should matter so much to Julia now?

She hardly expected to see Michael for some time, so she was most surprised when, only ten days later she heard that he had returned virtually unannounced.

"He phoned from Finnsport," explained his delighted mother, "to say that he wanted to be met from the next ferry. He was quite put out when Robert met him! I think he expected you!"

"Or, more probably, his car!" Julia smiled wryly, but Lady Barbara was bubbling with too much excitement to notice.

"He's a new person! Well — more like his old self, joke-a-minute, full of stories of his escapades with his wild friends, all those nightclubs! It's so wonderful to see him take an interest in things again."

Julia was a little puzzled. "Why has he come back here, then?"

"He seems to have some great master-plan in his mind. He wants to get himself really fit and strong while he's here — although I think he's almost better anyway. There's to be no more moping around anyway! He wants to invite some of his crowd here for a big end-of-season party, for fun and free publicity. He's just full of plans! I'm so hoping he'll stay on until Christmas and then — well I wouldn't expect to hold him much longer!"

With every word she heard, Julia's heart sank. This was a new man indeed, full of positive thinking and high spirits; a man who would simply use Rosa as a jumping-off point for his return to his own world.

"Will Michael be joining us for dinner?" she asked.

"Oh yes! He's over this 'recluse' phase, thank goodness!" His mother laughed with relief. She was usually sensitive to the younger woman's feelings but, today, the pleasure she was reaping from her son's return seemed, fortunately, to blind her to everything else.

At first, Julia accepted the 'new' Michael at face value. Over dinner that evening, and on meeting him at odd moments over the next few days, she found he was indeed in high spirits, entertaining anyone who cared to listen with tales of his raucous re-entry into 'the scene'. It seemed that for a fort-night he had been the life and soul of every society party in London! Everyone seemed to have been queueing up to welcome him!

Everything, in fact, was so marvellous as to be unbelievable! And, in the end, Julia found that she did not believe it. She looked at Michael, watched his eyes as she listened to another of his tales of gaudy night-life, and what she saw did not match the story. There was in his eyes a feverish excitement, almost like terror, which frightened her.

Certainly he had met up with his crowd again — she had seen the photographs! But something was ringing false. Michael might seem to be his old playboy self but Julia was sure it was an act; for what purpose she could not guess.

Where she herself was concerned Michael was unfailingly pleasant, so obviously 'nice', that Julia knew he was trying to re-state his case; that there was no future in any relationship with him. Now, it was up to her to accept it.

In his absence she had spent a lot of her spare time walking and exploring. It fascinated her to set off along a track and simply wait to see where it took her.

One evening she took a path she had never followed before, which, she suspected, led down to the shore below the estate. She was glad of her sturdy, flat shoes as she negotiated the twisting trail through bushes and trees. Suddenly she was in the open again, on a patch of rough long grass which sloped down towards a sandy beach. It was so tranquil, the late evening light soft and mellow. She had noticed before that the light fragrance of the island, the mingled scents of sea, sand and lush greenery, seemed to change in the evening after a warm summer day, becoming heady, rich and sensual.

She sat down on the grass, clasping her arms round her drawn-up knees, and watched the sea, its pattern constantly changing, yet somehow remaining the same.

She had been there, hypnotised by beauty, for some time when she became aware of movement on the beach, further along the shore, where sand dunes formed tiny valleys. At first she thought it might be some romantic holiday couple, but then a single figure emerged, and — instantly recognising the halting walk — she knew she must stay hidden.

Julia drew back against the trees; he would not notice her if she stayed put. She could not bear yet another confrontation with him, but it was growing darker and cooler every minute, and she hoped that he would soon pass, allowing her to make her escape.

As she looked again she could see that he was wearing a dark tracksuit. She wondered if he planned to swim as his specialist had advised, but he began to move, slowly at first, along the wet sand by the water's edge, gradually increasing speed to an awkward jogging pace. At once she realised what was happening here: he was trying to work on his fitness, get rid of the limp. And he was so afraid of the sympathy, or the pity, of those who loved him that he felt he had to carry out this battle alone.

As the thought passed through her mind, Julia finally accepted the truth. She was one of those who loved him. Why should she fight the inevitable? From the initial fascination, the challenge which his famed arrogance had presented to the strong young woman in her there had grown a love for this man which went far beyond that initial attraction. And now I'm spying on him, she thought, as she watched him jog back and forth, back and forth, along the sand. He was obviously tiring now, pushing himself too hard, and the limp became more and more pronounced until, to her concern, his weak leg seemed to give way under him and he collapsed by the shallow waves. She managed to resist the urge to rush to him, as he lay there, regaining his strength. Tears filled her eyes, and she clasped her hand over her mouth to stifle a sob. "Oh, my love!" she whispered. "My brave, dear love!" How she had misjudged him! How little allowance she had made for his suffering.

He lay there on the sand in the deepening gloom, apparently defeated, as she watched him. Then, just as she began to wonder if he were badly hurt, he clambered to his feet again, clutching his thigh, and began to hobble along the edge of the shore, stopping now and then to pick up stones to skim.

Julia knew that she must never let him find out that she had been present, that she had glimpsed the vulnerability beneath his strength. He was playing the part, for everyone, of the effortlessly recovering hero; outgoing, independent, devil-may-care. Privately he was struggling against pain, unwilling to ask for help, even for moral support. Julia was filled with love for him. She understood his pride, his need for self-esteem, this determination to keep secret his battle to return to full fitness.

Slowly she crept back towards the trees, determined that she must help him somehow, even if she had to use great tact and diplomacy. She felt happier than she had for weeks. Perhaps he might never return her love, but if she could do something positive to help him . . .

It became obvious during the following week that he worked on the beach each evening. Julia, suppressing the guilt she felt as she watched him from her hiding place in the trees, was pleased to see him make progress from day to day, increasing the time he spent running, or the strenuousness of the exercises. But instinctively she felt that she could help. If only she could tell him she knew, offer her unconditional support. Finally she decided on a make-or-break plan.

The evening was warm and still, perfect for a twilight swim. She had been careful to arrive earlier on the beach than Michael ever had, allowing him the opportunity to turn back when he saw her there.

The water was cold at first, but she was a strong swimmer and, as soon as she began to strike out, she enjoyed the tingling sensation of the water's coolness on her skin.

Her timing had been perfect for, when she stopped for breath, the figure was already by the water's edge. Pretending a cheeriness she did not truly feel, she raised her arm to wave, and then swam briskly towards him, where he stood by the sea's edge.

It was only as she stood up in the shallow that she noticed his look of admiration. Her black swimsuit was plain and figure-hugging, and her soaked hair was scraped back from her face. She could see from his expression that he was impressed, but this had not been her aim.

"What a beautiful evening!" she enthused. "Have you come to swim too? It's a super beach!"

"I . . ." he hesitated. "Well, yes, I thought I might, but . . ." She could see that he was uneasy, but a kind of fearlessness possessed her and she grasped his hands in hers.

"Oh do come in. It's such fun!" She turned away, running back through the waves until she could plunge into the coolness.

Her heart pounded in her ears. My God! How would he react? How had she dared? Suddenly she heard the sound behind her and he was there, his powerful arms bringing him through the water to her side.

They were both gasping for breath, and she laughed as she greeted him. "You swim well," he said, smiling at her. "I'm afraid I haven't been swimming for some time. And, of course, this is hardly an encouraging water temperature!" He laughed and splashed water at her, obviously enjoying the occasion. Apparently he suspected nothing untoward in her presence on this beach.

She began to swim and he joined her, noticeably holding back the power of his stroke to keep pace with her. When she stopped again for breath, she reached down to touch sand and discovered she was just out of her depth. She gave an involuntary gasp and immediately his arms encircled her clasping Julia to him with a fierceness and protectiveness which thrilled her. Their bodies were drawn together in the cool darkness of the water, and desire for him rushed through her. Supporting her uplifted head with his powerful hand, he gently kissed her wet cheeks. She closed her eyes, melting into the sensation of his mouth upon hers, the taste of salt on his lips. She drifted against him, so sure of his strength, his power.

The tide carried them in towards the shore. As her toes touched the sand, and she regained her balance, he suddenly released her and, relaxing on to his back, swam away from her, his eyes still fixed on her face. She realised that she felt chilled now, and almost unreal. She turned towards the shore and ran up to the dunes where her towel lay. Clutching it around her she watched him swim to shore and gather his own clothes.

He was wearing only briefs and she could see the livid scarring on his leg as he came towards her, but his physique was powerful and heavily muscled.

"Here!" she said. "Use this," and she held out towards him the extra towel she had brought with her.

"Were you a Girl Guide?" he laughed. "Always prepared for an unexpected guest?"

"You weren't unexpected, Michael." She had done it, had burned her boats. "I know you come here in the evenings, and I know why." He turned away, his face full of anger.

"No, Michael, please! Don't be angry. I truly want to help you. Please let me help you." She pleaded for all she was worth. "I could work with you, keep you going, offer you a bit of moral support. Why do you have to do this on your own? Why won't you let anyone help you?"

He was furiously drying himself but at her final words he turned on her, grasping her bare arm so tightly it hurt.

"I'm so tired of pity!" he said, spitting the words at her. "I can fight my own battles. Why don't you just leave me alone?" He sat down heavily on the sand and looked at her. Julia became acutely aware that she was wrapped only in a towel and her face flushed. He responded to her embarrassment. "You take a lot of risks, Julia. Coming here alone, leaving nothing to imagination in that swimsuit. What are you really after, goody-two-shoes?" Suddenly he moved nearer, throwing her back on the sand. Leaning over he kissed her without affection. Julia tried to push him off, but he only laughed at her. "Oh, come now! Don't play the foolish virgin with me. What you want, is what you get!"

His lips sought her neck, her ears, her

mouth, but he was rough and cruel. Julia felt afraid: there was something in his mood she could not understand. He was trying to punish her and he was using physical passion as his weapon. But she was even more frightened by the reaction of her own body, which burned to surrender to him.

His hands moved possessively over her, pulling, dragging at the towel until inevitably it fell away and she was naked under his touch. His body pressed against hers, crushing her, and she was aware that he was ready to take full advantage of his power over her.

Suddenly tears welled in her eyes and, to her own surprise, she let out a sob of anguish.

"Leave me alone, Michael!" she cried, trying to wrench her wrists free of his grasp.

To her astonishment he pulled away from her, throwing himself back on the sand as she hastily pulled the towel around her, trying to stifle her sobs. He was breathing heavily still, his arm thrown up as though to shield his eyes.

"Julia!" he whispered. "I'm sorry . . . I thought . . ."

"No, you didn't think! You never think, Michael! Do I really seem to you the kind of woman who wants that sort of treatment? You're right — I am a foolish virgin!" But she knew that she was not being strictly honest. Even if he had again been acting a part, her own confused physical responses had been real. She had wanted him, but she had also wanted him to care.

"Julia . . ." He turned to her again as he stood to dress.

"No, don't say any more, Michael. I didn't want it to be like this. All I want is to help you. I'm not asking anything in return. If you can't believe that, I'm sorry."

They both dressed in silence. He seemed drained now, shocked by his miscalculation of her motives, but exhausted too by his swim. The anger and hurt Julia had felt quickly evaporated.

"Will you come back to the Lodge — for coffee, no strings?" Michael asked, so meekly that Julia agreed. She looked at him, wondering what he was thinking now. He had been genuinely shocked by his own behaviour, she believed. He had assumed that she had had lovers before, and was simply trying to seduce him. Was he so used to women of that sort that on two occasions he had accused her of being one of them? Had he never been truly loved before? She wanted to tell of her love but could not. So often in her teenage years her aunt had counselled her not to wear her heart on her sleeve. Seeing her niece's eyes bright with adoration for some spotty sixth-former she would warn her of the benefits of remaining 'aloof and mysterious'. It had not been Julia's way then, nor was it now. But she could not burden Michael with the knowledge of her love.

As they walked back towards the Lodge he took her hand and lifted it to his lips. "I'm sorry," he said. "I seem to spend all my time apologising to you." He shook his head sadly. "There is no excuse for treating you so badly. But if I could tell you how confused I feel sometimes."

Julia sensed that he needed to talk. This incident between them had forced a crisis in their relationship, but it had made him analyse his own feelings. Later, as he lay stretched out on one of the couches before the Lodge's beautiful fire, she listened in silence as he tried to explain himself.

"I look in the mirror, Julia, and I see this," he indicated the scar, "and it isn't me. It isn't my face any more. I know it's vanity, I know! But how can I stop myself feeling like that? And what use am I to anyone or anything while I'm crippled by this leg? I used to be so fit, I took it for granted. Even after the accident, I didn't really believe them when they told me how long and how

hard I'd have to exercise to recover fully —
if I ever did."

His blue eyes were deeply troubled as he
looked at her. "Julia. I know you think you
— think you're fond of me. But pity is a
strange thing, it can seem to be something
it isn't." She made to protest, but he was
not ready to listen. "You shouldn't be wast-
ing your time on me. You deserve a man
who can love you in return, a kind, gentle
man who would cherish you and care for
you. I'm all wrong for you — I want to be
your friend, but if you want more of me, I
can't give it."

"I love you," she whispered.

"No — no, you're sorry for me, sweet Julia. And that is something entirely different.
In any case I don't know what love is. It's
an emotion I have never experienced."

Julia gazed into the leaping flames. Should
she believe him? How could someone be
unable to love? The idea seemed ridiculous
to her.

"I won't ask anything of you, Michael.
What I feel really doesn't matter. All I want
is to see you strong and fit again. Then
you'll be able to go back to your world."

He stared at her, as though he could not
believe that anyone could offer herself
without a price-tag. He sat up, his eyes still

fixed on her, reading her expression, and held out his hands toward her.

"It's a deal! If you really mean it, you crazy girl, why should I turn down your offer?" He made it sound like a business arrangement. "And in return I'll try to be less, shall we say, troublesome!"

Julia glowed with happiness. This man, so dear to her, would accept her help. She would hope for no more, but even this was very special to her.

"Now!" he said, a boyish smile playing on his handsome face. "Shall we plan our training programme, coach?"

In the weeks which followed, the two spent every spare moment together. Michael began to drive again, still with some discomfort at first, but the boost to his morale of driving the beautiful car made any minor difficulty worthwhile. Twice a week they drove the ten miles to the island's only indoor pool. Julia, now well used to the blend of praise and bullying he needed to spur him on, would watch as he swam further and further on each visit. Finally exhausted he would clamber out, panting and laughing, delighted with another personal victory, to where she waited with a huge towel.

At such times as these, try as she might, she could not suppress the warm surge of physical desire she felt for him. His body had grown lean and tanned over the weeks and the constant well-planned exercise had begun to develop even further the muscles of his back, his arms and his powerful thighs, making their contours more clearly defined. But she was able to accept her desire for him now and was not ashamed that her love for him should express itself thus. It was quite natural after all and she loved him more each day, sharing his exultation at each step towards strength.

Even more important was his returning confidence. As he began to notice his own progress he became more relaxed, even letting his mother and brother share the 'secret' of his activities.

Julia continued to give full attention to her work at the castle, but as soon as she was off duty she would rush to change and meet Michael, to jog with him round the estate's roadways or to review the training schedule for the coming week.

Lady Barbara had watched the change in the relationship and finally, after a business meeting, she broached the subject.

"I'm so happy for Michael. His progress is so rapid now; and I know we have you to thank for that." She hesitated, and Julia sensed her unease. "I don't know how to put this, my dear, but I feel I have to say it — for your sake. I know you have grown very fond of my son, and I know too that he owes you a great deal. But you must be prepared, child. I am sure he intends to return to London quite soon. He has been in touch with many of his friends, including Miss O'Brienn, and he seems to be telling them all that he'll be back soon." She faltered, but Julia fixed a quiet smile on her face in reply.

"I appreciate your concern, Lady Barbara, but I promise you I am aware of Michael's plans. I'm under no illusions about his feelings for me: I think he has grown quite fond of me as a friend and helper, but I know there cannot be any more to it than that."

Lady Barbara seemed convinced by Julia's calm response, and they concluded their meeting without mentioning Michael again.

As August drew to a close and everyone began to look forward to the end of their first, hectic season as a tourist attraction, Michael decided to invite Robert, his mother and Julia to supper at the Lodge, to celebrate as he put it, his 'return' to the world. It was the greatest mark of his recovery that he had grown less inclined to hide away, and they all shared his pleasure in his remarkable progress.

Not content with preparing a magnificent cassoulet, he insisted that they all inspect the luxury kitchen in which he had created it.

"It's such a pity, though," he said as he demonstrated all the fitments and gadgets, "I've just got used to the oven and the dishwasher and everything, and I'll be leaving it all behind! Never mind, it'll be ideal for holidays, if I find time to fit them in."

"You've definitely decided to return to the bright lights, then?" enquired Robert.

"I'll be back quite frequently. But really, London's a much better base for me. It's more my style, I suppose, after all this time away from home, and all my friends are there."

Their discussion was halted for some time by the serving of the delicious meal, but Robert was determined to pursue the matter of Michael's future.

"I was hoping you might consider staying, taking on the tourist business," he explained. "It would leave me more time to concentrate on agricultural development."

"Oh, come on, Rob! You can cope. Especially now you've got Julia to help you.

Heavens, she could run the castle on her own!"

He smiled at her and her heart leaped, as it always did in response to any sign of his approval. "She's a gem!" he went on, "A hard taskmistress, but a good one. I'd still be hobbling around like an old wreck if she hadn't taken me in hand!"

As though sensing the young woman's embarrassment, his mother broke in, "But we haven't even asked Julia what her plans are! There will be some loose ends to tie up after we close to the public, and I'd really like to know she was in charge while Robert and I were away." She turned to Julia. "But after that, dear, you must decide for yourself. I would like to think you would stay on with us permanently; after a holiday, of course!"

It was the first time they had discussed this and Julia did not reply immediately.

Misunderstanding her silence, Lady Barbara went on: "Of course, I understand that Rosa in the depths of winter may not be everyone's cup of tea. But you must think it over, and let us know what you decide."

It was a happy evening, which they all enjoyed. As they left Michael took Julia aside. "I think you'd like life here, Julia. And I'd feel much happier, knowing Robert and mother had you to rely on while I'm gone."

Perhaps so, thought Julia. But how can I be happy, here or anywhere, without you?

Six

She looked forward to the end of the castle's open season with a mixture of pleasure and regret. The venture had been an undoubted success and they had all learned a great deal about tourism and dealing with the public, which would stand them in good stead in future years. Already Lady Barbara was considering an extended season, opening earlier to catch the Easter visitors. Julia felt uneasy at such discussion, for she still had not decided what she would do.

And always at the back of her mind was the knowledge that her precious time with Michael would soon be over. In all the weeks they had worked together to improve his fitness he had been kind, friendly and openly grateful. Often, he had laughed at her earnestness as she spurred him on to yet another length of the pool, or another jog along the sand, and he seemed at least to have accepted that she truly wanted to help him. But there had been no hint of love in his words or actions. He was careful never to touch her, beyond the occasional playful slap on the back, or a gentle punch in retaliation for her relentless supervision of his training.

At night, after spending an evening with him, she would lie awake, reliving every moment when he could so easily have touched or held her had he wanted to, finally accepting that his behaviour was not a display of self-restraint but, rather, a lack of desire.

Sometimes she felt she would die of longing for some small sign that, miraculously, he had grown to want her as she wanted him. But there never was such a sign. I am finding out, she thought, what love really is; loving him so much that I am working to make him strong enough to leave me!

Although she had helped in mailing invitations and contacting local caterers Julia had had comparatively little to do with the organisation of the party. Most of Michael's guests would be staying at the largest of the local hotels, reassured by its four 'stars', and it seemed that they intended to make the party the highlight of an autumn holiday, waiting on afterwards for a week of socialising with their set. Michael talked with satisfaction of drawing his group into the autumn social calendar in Scotland, already so popular with the Royal Family.

Julia herself had invited her cousin Anne, who would arrive in time for the party, and stay on at the castle for a fortnight to keep Julia company in Lady Barbara's absence. It was Anne's first visit to Scotland and Julia looked forward to showing her around this beautiful island.

Guests began to arrive on the day before the party. The local garage was soon doing a roaring trade, taxiing rich young socialites between the Highland Hotel and the Lodge. Julia was instructed to meet the late afternoon ferry with Robert, to welcome some of the older guests, friends of Lady Barbara. As they drew up at the pier carpark she noticed Michael's car, and as she and Robert walked to meet the approaching ferry, they could hear the sounds of laughter and shouts from its fore deck as a group of bright young things made their first contact with their host, who stood waving to them from the pier.

Julia watched, stricken with misery, as several photographers jostled each other at the foot of the gangway, cameras clicking wildly as Michael's guests appeared.

Their clothes, their voices, their self-confidence and extrovert jollity, all spoke of money and social position. They glittered and shone amongst their anorak-ed and business-suited fellow passengers.

Finally a very pretty woman with fashionably wild, blonde hair and unbelievably figure-hugging designer jeans, rushed down the gangway and straight into Michael's arms. As he lifted her, and whirled her round, almost knocking the photographers flying, his friends yelled and applauded their approval of the dazzling couple. "Darling, darling Michael!" the blonde cried, beating elegant fists on Michael's powerful shoulders. "Stop it, you absolute terror!"

Julia felt Robert's hand squeeze her arm. "Kerrin O'Brienn," he whispered. "What is known in the trade as 'just a good friend'!" And immediately Julia recognised the young woman who had appeared with Michael in the newspaper photograph. She was even more beautiful in real life, thought Julia, dismayed at her own jealousy.

At that moment Robert spotted the elderly couple they had been sent to meet and she had little opportunity to watch the antics of Michael's crowd. But later as she drove off she saw Kerrin, sitting in the silver Mercedes, locked in what appeared to be the most passionate embrace with Michael.

Lady Barbara's friends and Miss O'Brienn

were the only guests who would dine at the castle that evening. Julia dressed with special care but as she looked in the mirror she was depressed by the thought that Kerrin would outshine everyone else present.

How could she survive the evening? The man she loved would be there, with the gorgeous woman described in newspapers at the time of the accident as his 'girlfriend'. What sort of euphemism was that in a modern world? Perhaps Kerrin was the real reason for Michael's determined independence at the Lodge. After all, thought Julia bitterly, it would be hard to set up a love-nest with your mistress under your mother's roof, even if, technically, you owned the roof.

She was appalled at the way in which her imagination conjured up pictures of the lovers together. She ached for Michael's touch, and to think of him making love to someone else was torture! But what right had she to behave like this? Michael could not have made it more clear that he did not love her, that he saw her only as an employee and friend. Yet here she was, acting as though she had some right to be possessive. In reality he had rejected her time after time.

She was trembling as she paused at the door of the lounge, hearing the animated conversation within.

"Come along now, Julia! Too timid to enter?" Michael's voice, so close behind, startled her.

He ushered her into the room, his hand resting lightly on her elbow. "Let me introduce you to my very special guest — Kerrin O'Brienn, this is Julia Markman; I believe she is what is known as 'Girl Friday' to my mother, and a positive treasure to us all." His tone was laced with irony, and his grip on her elbow had become so tight that it hurt. What was he doing? Was he mocking her, insulting her, making sure that she was quite aware of her place in the scheme of things?

She glanced up at him, but his gaze was fixed on the lovely face of his guest.

"Ah, yes! This is your 'coach', Michael?" The actress extended a bejewelled hand. "My dear girl, you've worked absolute wonders with your protegé. He seems to be super-fit again; thanks, I hear, to you." Julia dredged a smile from her misery and was grateful when attention was distracted from her by the announcement that dinner was served.

Kerrin O'Brienn was a rising star in the film world, her face already gracing the covers of prestigious magazines, a sure sign of celebrity. She was, Julia had to admit, beautiful. Her tumbling blonde hair was caught back in combs from her face, revealing exquisite features daringly accentuated by a skilled hand. Her gown was rather more formal than normally worn for dinner here, its clinging white jersey and unique cut revealing every curve of a body well-known to filmgoers. As Julia had feared, her own dress of pale turquoise seemed almost dowdy in comparison but, she decided, it was probably best to merge into the crowd, play an extra's part.

During dinner she watched Kerrin dazzle everyone. The young woman had a pretty laugh and was full of stories of the famous 'names' with whom she had worked. She charmed everyone, particularly the men. Michael leaned back in his chair at the head of the table, the perfect model of the genial host, dispersing good humour and pleasant conversation.

Julia tried to read his expression as he looked at Kerrin. Was he in love with her, she wondered. She certainly seemed to worship him, for her stories and anecdotes were littered with 'Michael said' and 'I told Michael'. He must, at the very least, be flattered by the adoration of such a beautiful and vivacious young woman.

It seemed to Julia that Michael had drifted from her in some way. The actress's presence, and the arrival of his social set, had taken him away from her, as though all the time they had spent together had been just a dream.

She knew that sleep would be impossible for her for hours yet and when the dinner guests began to retire, she slipped away and quickly changed into jeans and jacket. Walking had become a special comfort for her since her arrival on Rosa, and this evening she made her way down towards the shore where she had worked so often with Michael. The moon was bright, casting a shimmering causeway of light across the wide bay. As so often before, she wondered at the bewitching beauty of the island. She picked up handfuls of pebbles and tried to skim them across the moonlit waters.

"You're still hopeless!" Michael's voice reached her from the edge of the woodland where he sat, crouched to watch her as she had once watched him. She did not reply, but continued to throw stones. "Improving," he murmured, reaching her side and joining her in stone-skimming.

"Shouldn't you be entertaining your guests?" she asked casually.

"Oh, I should think they'll be quite able

to look after themselves. The hotel was importing a disco this evening, especially for them."

"And Miss O'Brienn?"

"Kerrin goes early to bed — actresses, you know, must protect their assets!"

Julia sighed. "She's so lovely. If I thought a few early nights would make me look like that . . ."

Michael stopped skimming stones and gazed at her, as though puzzled. "Why on earth should you want to look like Kerrin? She's very pretty, I accept, and she knows how to make the most of her looks. But you are a very attractive woman. Why try to copy when you can be the original?"

How could she speak the answer which sprang to mind; that she wanted him to cherish her as he seemed to cherish Kerrin? Instead she shrugged it off with a little laugh.

"Don't be too impressed by what is on the outside," he went on, quite serious now. "Kerrin herself is a good person, but not all of the glamorous crowd you'll meet at our party are really nice to know. Some of them, I don't like at all." He was emphatic.

"Then why on earth did you invite them?"

"What a very good question. I wish I knew the answer to that one." He smiled and her heart melted. "Perhaps I've changed after all." His tone was wistful, as though this thought had not occurred to him before.

She was surprised when he suggested a nightcap at the Lodge.

"But Miss O'Brienn?"

"Oh, she's not staying at the Lodge! Heavens, you don't think you'd catch Kerrin roughing it with one shower, half-installed central heating and no slaves!"

Julia tried to conceal what she felt at this revelation and politely refused his invitation. But when she had left him she could barely stifle a cry of delight. She was embarrassed by her elation at the discovery that Kerrin was not to spend the night at the Lodge! She rebuked herself, reasoning that Michael was quite capable of being with Kerrin in her rooms at the castle; this was hardly something to celebrate as a personal victory. And yet, it felt so good.

She was rather taken aback then, to encounter Kerrin on the landing leading to the guest rooms.

"Can I help you, Miss O'Brienn?" she stammered.

"Please call me Kerrin! Actually, I was just going to creep down to the kitchens in search of a pot of tea."

Julia immediately offered to fetch some

for the woman and was invited to join her. Kerrin was brushing her hair when she returned with the tray.

"How how kind of you! I find it so hard to get to sleep — especially alone! But tea is a substitute for lots of things!" Julia blushed at the suggestiveness of the remark, but the young woman seemed not to notice. "I seem to have been 'boarded out'! Michael insists that the Lodge isn't suitable for guests yet. What sort of hovel is it, I ask myself." Julia could not reply, stricken as she was with something akin to panic at this different version of the lovers' separation.

"I think he's changed, you know," Kerrin went on, as though chatting to a close friend. "I know him better than most, and I think he's quite strange at the moment. Time to get him back to London permanently, I think!" She chatted on, mentioning names and places which Julia knew only from the society pages of *Harper's* and *Queen*. At last it seemed an opportune moment to excuse herself and return to the privacy of her own room, and the bewildering array of emotions which churned inside her.

There was little point in pretending that she did not care. It mattered greatly to her that Michael had not wanted Kerrin to be with him at the Lodge. It was, after all, some small comfort.

"You romantic idiot! You're potty about him, aren't you?" Anne demanded, as they shared lunch in Julia's room the following day.

Julia giggled. " 'Potty about'! You make it sound like *Girl's Own Paper,* or the Chalet School."

"Come on, don't dodge the issue. You must tell all to your understanding cousin," Anne pursued, determined to share the secret.

It was such a relief to have someone to confide in at last that Julia poured everything out; her confusion, her hurt, her love for him. By the time she was finished she had been talking for nearly two hours. Anne was silent for a while, anxiety clouding her expression.

"Jools, love —" she said at last, "are you sure you really love him? No — don't get all upset. But Mother always says you can't really experience love unless you're getting some sort of response. And it sounds to me . . ." She paused, not wishing to be damaging. "Look, I just don't want you to get hurt, and I know you will be!"

Julia shrugged her shoulders. She knew

that Anne's honesty sprang from genuine concern but, equally, she was sure of her feelings.

"How can I stop myself, Anne? I know what he is, and I know he doesn't want me, but I look at him and — I'm lost!"

"Oh do take care, girl. A man like that doesn't know what a woman's love is worth. He'll use you, treat you like a commodity, and it won't hurt him one bit. I think it'll do you good to get away from here for a while."

"Anyway — enough of m'Lord Michael! What am I going to wear to this shindig, then?" Soon they were laughing and giggling over their preparations for the party, just as they had done as happy teenagers.

When they came downstairs that evening the banqueting hall was already filling with guests and the band, darlings of Michael's crowd, had begun to play.

"Look at these frocks!" whispered Anne. "I thought they only existed on the pages of *Vogue*." She was not exaggerating. The debs, ex-debs, glitterati, aspiring talents, had spent a fortune in the race to be the most fashionable. Julia was glad of the classic elegance of her Parisian gown, and was quite pleased with her own appearance.

Anne, wide-eyed with admiration, was

happy just to observe, and soon was drawn into conversation with Lady Barbara and her guests. Julia found herself chatting dutifully to endless strangers, inevitably recalling Michael's strange assessment of his friends.

True, some of them did seem affected and brittle, their eyes roaming over the room while their mouths talked to Julia, always looking for someone more interesting. But many of them seemed quite genuine and Julia mingled with them, pleased to enjoy their fun-filled company.

People strayed off to the buffet tables, and dancing began. Julia, never lacking a partner, was whisked round the floor by a succession of elegant young men.

Occasionally she caught sight of Michael, always the centre of a group of admirers, but she had not spoken to him when, finally, he asked her to dance.

The music for once was slow and dreamy, and as he took her in his arms she glowed with happiness. It was a very strange, but sensual experience; held close to him, the top of her head reaching only to his chin, she felt warm and protected. When he wanted to talk to her he was obliged to bend, to speak close in her ear, and she could smell the cologne on his warm skin.

She ached to touch his face, his hair, to kiss him. It was exquisite torture to be so close to him and not be able to do so.

Before the music had ended, however, he took her hand. "Come with me, I have something to show you." She was aware of many eyes following them as he led her out through the high french windows and towards the driveway, where the Mercedes stood.

"Isn't this rather rude? What about your guests?"

"I couldn't care less, Julia!"

"But where are we going?"

"The Lodge. I have something there for you." He said nothing more during the short drive and Julia tried to read his mood from his silence.

When he opened the door, the room was lit by the warm glow of the logfire. He switched on one of the lamps and sat down.

"Come here to me." He indicated where she was to sit. "I wanted to see you privately because I may not get the chance to again, before we all go our separate ways. I had to thank you for what you've done for me." He took her hands in his, and Julia's heart stopped. "I know I would never have worked so hard without you to drive me on, make me believe in myself again."

"I was glad to help. I . . ." How could she say that she had done it with love, that she adored him? She could not risk breaking the spell, the magic of these moments alone with him.

"I want you to have this," he said, reaching for a box which lay on the table by his side. "Take care — it's very fragile!"

Julia lifted the lid and gently removed soft tissue paper. She glanced at him in disbelief. It was a delicate porcelain figure, very similar to the one which Michael had told her was his favourite. The figure was of a girl in a blue gown, a coronet of tiny flowers in her hair.

"I can't possibly accept . . ."

"You must! You must, I want you to have it." He spoke very firmly and Julia knew she could not refuse him. She leaned forward to kiss his cheek in thanks but as her lips touched the line of the scar which still showed there he took the box from her and replaced it on the table. His hands encircled her face and their lips met. For those few moments the world ceased to exist for her. The taste and smell of him, the intoxicating sense of the power behind the gentleness with which his mouth moved upon hers, drew her inwards as though she had been merged with him. She lifted her hand to touch his hair, the nape of his neck, the broad strength of his shoulders, and she knew that she would willingly give him everything if he were to show the slightest sign that he wanted her.

But she could sense no fiery passion in his lingering kiss, only a terrible sadness, a heartbreaking sense of a last goodbye to her. Finally she could bear no more and she drew apart from him, somehow contriving to smile. They both knew that their time together was over, and moments like these simply prolonged the pain for her.

"Shouldn't we go back?" she asked quietly, and he nodded wearily.

They drove back in silence, Michael returning to his guests while Julia took his precious gift to her room. As she climbed the stairs she was shocked to discover Kerrin, on the landing, gazing up at the portrait of Michael.

"It's breathtaking isn't it?" said Kerrin. "It's so awful that he's scarred for life. He really was gorgeous!"

"Was!" Julia was appalled. "I think he's still the most handsome man I've ever met — more so now. That portrait makes him look so perfect he seems cold and unreachable. He's just not like that." She had not meant to say so much, but she was defensive of Michael.

The actress turned towards her, her eyes suddenly alight with discovery. "You're in love with him, aren't you?" Julia looked away, her cheeks on fire. "I can see you are," went on Kerrin. "It's in your eyes every time you look at him." There was no malice in her voice as she spoke. "I wish you luck, Julia, but for your own sake, I have to warn you. Michael isn't a man who gives. He will take, but he is lord of his own heart, and in absolute control. Perhaps he truly is unreachable. I don't know if he could love anyone." She touched Julia's arm lightly in a gesture of sympathy and went downstairs.

Julia went on to her room, stunned by the young woman's frankness. She sat for some time, regaining what composure she could muster, before opening the box once more. This time, she noticed a folded note, tucked at the side of the figurine. In Michael's hand were written the words: *To my dear friend, Julia, who cared for me.* Tears filled her eyes as she quickly refolded the paper. Had he ever understood just how much she cared? Did he know that every time she looked at the porcelain figure, her heart would be with him, wherever he was?

SEVEN

The following day Lady Barbara and Robert departed for London. While his mother intended to fly on to the South of France for a long vacation Robert was to spend only a fortnight with friends in London before returning to resume control of the castle. He assured Julia that Michael, although busy with the group of his friends who were staying on Rosa for the coming week, would at least be 'around', should she need him. Julia suppressed the ironic smile prompted by his well-meaning remark.

"In any case," she insisted, "I have Anne here for moral support. And I'm sure nothing will happen that we'll need to worry about."

Robert, finally convinced that she would phone him in any emergency, accepted her assurances that he could enjoy his holiday with no thought of his responsibilities here.

There was plenty to do at first, with the

cleaning-up after the party to be supervised and the castle's final few paying visitors to be looked after. The cousins rather enjoyed being in command. During the second week, however, with the castle closed and all but the regular staff on leave of absence for the winter they had time to tour the island and absorb its atmosphere.

"The locals say that Rosa is at her best at this time of year," mused Julia, and it was not hard to see why.

The quality of light had changed subtly as though to complement the autumn golds and russets. Where in summer there had been wide swathes of uniform greenery, there now reappeared contour and texture, in endless changes of colour and tone. Even the sea seemed different, its colour changing minute by minute as it reflected the wind-tossed clouds which scudded across the sky. And everywhere on the island there was the smell of wood-smoke — not acrid like a city bonfire, but spicy, mysterious.

" 'Season of mists and mellow fruitfulness'," quoted Anne, returning to schooldays for an adequate response to the glory of the island's autumn.

They had borrowed the Land Rover each day, travelling to points from which they could explore on foot, or simply sit and watch the sea. Everywhere, the island was changing gear for the winter. Small hotels were closing, cafes putting up their shutters, beach huts had been removed, and camp sites restored to the care of the sheep and cattle. The yachts which had bobbed in the island's increasingly-busy marina were all safely ashore now, pathetically inelegant behind their high mesh fences, like stranded swans. The locals, who had worked so hard during the summer season, seemed almost excited at the prospect of reclaiming their island for a few months and notices appeared in shop windows advertising the restarting of a variety of social groups.

"It's like Sleeping Beauty," remarked Anne. "Or an animal going into hibernation. And then, in Spring, it'll all come to life again. Do you think you'll stay on?"

"Lady B and Robert certainly want me to and, if Michael goes, it should be less awkward for me. After all, why should I leave? I love the work, and we've got so many ideas for next year. And anyway the island has me firmly in its spell — Robert warned me I'd get 'hooked'!" Time after time this summer she had spoken to visitors who had spent every holiday on Rosa for twenty, thirty years. They all spoke of its magical ability to capture the heart, and it had undoubtedly captured Julia's.

"Well," reasoned Anne, "you'll have a chance to get things into perspective while you're home." How strange, Julia thought, that it was no longer London that she considered *home.*

Although Michael had often been in their thoughts and conversation in the past few days they had seen very little of him. On several occasions as they toured the island the girls had seen his car parked outside the island's golf club, or one of the little pubs or coffee shops still open, as he and his friends continued to enjoy an autumn holiday in right royal style, leaving the locals agog and providing a plentiful supply of anecdotes to be told and retold in the long winter evenings which lay ahead.

One morning several days before Robert was due to return Michael appeared at the castle for breakfast, to 'beg a favour', he warned. His guests had all gone, 'at last', he told them, and he was glad to see the back of them.

"Not very generous of you, mine host!" Julia teased, enjoying the opportunity of chatting with him in circumstances which were not emotionally loaded.

"Just a case of too much of a good thing," he responded in mock exhaustion. "I have to admit I am out of practice. I don't know how I ever kept up that pace."

"You'll soon be into the way of it again, I should think," Anne remarked pointedly, but Michael was not forthcoming. Presumably he had not yet fixed the date of his departure from Rosa. Now, he was going to have a few days to himself.

"And the favour?" asked Julia.

"Oh, nothing much. Just a lift in the Range Rover, actually." It transpired that he planned to spend the day on the hills. He would walk through Glen Mhor, probably the most awesome of the island's beautiful glens with its sheer rock faces towering over the rough moorland and the valleys below. It seemed a good day for it he thought. Could Julia and Anne help by driving him to the point at which he would start?

Julia agreed readily, but she felt a twinge of concern. Many of the island's holiday-makers came to try the splendid hill walks, which ranged from rambles suitable for young children to challenging climbs for the more experienced. 'The Crags', as the central section of the route through Glen Mhor was known, was recognised as the most difficult on the island. Michael had certainly done it in the past, before his accident, but he had done no serious walking since. She was not sure that his plan was very wise, and yet if she were to voice her doubts he would react very badly, she knew. There was nothing for it but to bite her tongue and hope that his understandable desire to meet the challenge had not over-ruled his common sense.

Following the plan of most experienced walkers Michael drove his own car to the end of the path from Glen Mhor nearest to home, before travelling with Julia and Anne to his starting point several miles to the north.

He was well equipped and so patently eager to prove that he could do it that Julia permitted herself only a whispered, "Take care!" as she waved goodbye to him. Her concern, however, was all too plain to Anne.

"You're worried about him, aren't you? Don't you think he's ready for this walk?"

"Anne, it's the most difficult one he could have chosen! Oh, I'm just being over-protective, clucking like a mother hen," Julia laughed, but her heart was heavy. He would be furious if he knew. "Come on! Let's go back to that little tearoom we passed. I could do with a cuppa!"

But Julia could not laugh off her fears so easily. What had been a fine clear morning suddenly changed to a grey rain-drenched afternoon, and a brisk wind began to pick up. Trying not to voice her concern, she busied herself washing and ironing those clothes she would need on holiday, but her eyes constantly strayed to the clock.

"He'll be all right!" Anne reassured her. "He knows how quickly the weather changes at this time of year, and he knows the route well enough."

"I know, I know! But he hasn't really tested his leg like this before, and it's such a hard climb near the top of The Crags. I've read about it in the guidebook." She knew that these books always stressed the difficulties of a walk in order to discourage the inexperienced but already this summer police and forest rangers had issued warnings about the dangerous state of some of the higher sections of rough path through Glen Mhor.

The minutes and hours crawled by. Michael had agreed to join them for dinner, and when he had not arrived at 7.30, Julia 'phoned the Lodge. There was no reply, and her fears were immediately multiplied.

"Perhaps he's in the shower," Anne reasoned, trying to calm her cousin, but despite herself growing anxious that some accident had indeed occurred.

"You stay here." Julia was decisive. "I'll go

134

down to the Lodge, and if he isn't there, I'll go on up to the farm and fetch Donny Macfarlane and his boys. I know he's probably just late, but I must make sure."

It was dusk as she drove from the castle. The wind was strong now, and rattled the rain fiercely against the Range Rover's windows. The Lodge was in darkness, no car parked there. Taking a deep breath, Julia decided that she would be of no use to anyone if she panicked. She drove as fast as she could to the Macfarlanes' where she hastily explained everything to Donny.

"What the hell does he think he's aboot?" growled Donny, not a man to mince words. "Yon's no' a walk for a man that's just got himsel' better! There's dozens o' other walks he could've tried!" But his kind, weather-beaten face mirrored Julia's own concern and, quickly calling his two strapping sons, he took over the wheel of the Range Rover, driving with all the speed and skill of an expert.

The Mercedes stood where it had been parked. "No damn guid a car like that!" Donny was scathing. "OK for the city, too pretty for these tracks. Guid job we brought this." Abrupt though his manner was Julia could tell that he too was deeply worried now.

Darkness was falling as they drove up the impossibly narrow and rocky hill path. After half a mile of bone-shaking, Donny stopped. "We'll no' get any further in this. Right, lass! You're to stay here in case the silly fool makes it back under his own steam. If he does, just blast the horn. Right lads, let's go and get his Lordship!" They strode off into the darkness, only their torches casting light on the silvery needles of rain.

Julia was left alone, hugging herself with worry on the cramped front seat. She looked at her watch — a quarter to nine.

The waiting was unbearable. Her heart seemed made of lead, and her mouth was dry with fear. The silence roared in her ears until she wanted to talk to herself just to hear a voice. Her imagination raced ahead of her reason. In her mind's eye she saw him lying crumpled in some gully. Then a wave of anger swept away her fear: why did he have to be so stubborn, so stupidly determined to prove himself? Why did men feel they had always to be proving their physical strength?

No sooner was her fury at full flood than remorse and guilt replaced it. How could she be angry with him when he might be lying out there . . . ?

She sat there shivering as much with apprehension as with cold, until she could stand it no longer. She knew she must stay by the Range Rover, but it seemed a fraud to be dry and safe when the others were out on the hills. She clambered out, into pouring rain and a chill wind which seemed to be funnelled by the Glen's steep sides. She paced up and down, talking to herself, tears of fear and frustration mixing with the rain on her cheeks, for what felt like hours.

As it turned out it was only ten o'clock when she glimpsed the flicker of a torch beam through the gloom and heard Donny's gruff call. "We've got him, Miss! But he's in some mess!" Julia's fears turned to relief as the Macfarlane boys appeared, chairing Michael between them. They had found him just a mile or so up the path. He had slipped on the high stretch of The Crags and wrenched his weak leg very badly but somehow he had managed to force himself on, experience telling him to keep to the known path all the time.

Now, he was on the verge of collapse; his face, scratched and mud-splattered, was contorted with pain. They lifted him as gently as they could into the back of the Range Rover, where Julia covered him with sacking and blankets which Donny had wisely brought.

"Best if you stop at the bottom o' this path and take his car, Miss. You can go on ahead an' get the doctor. We'll get young Michael here up to the Lodge House." Big Donny patted her head. "It's OK lass. You did well, and he'll be just fine, silly devil though he is!"

When she arrived at the Lodge, the doctor following close behind, Donny and his sons were just leaving. They told her they had got Michael into bed and had lit the fire. Julia thanked them for all they had done and, remembering Anne, asked them to stop at the castle to tell her what had occurred.

She stripped off her soaking jacket and sweater and, wrapping herself in the tartan rug from the car, she heated up some soup in an effort to drive the chill from her bones. Even crouched by the fire she felt that she would never be warm again.

"He's totally exhausted and very shaken," Doctor Menteith told her when he left the bedroom some time later. "But I've checked him over, and I don't think there's any lasting damage to the leg. He was in a fair bit of pain so I've given him something to relax the muscles, help him get to sleep. He's pretty groggy now — can you get someone down to keep an eye on him overnight?" Julia promised that she would.

"You look exhausted yourself, my girl! Better get out of those damp things and into a warm bath."

The bedroom was lit only by the small bedside lamp. Michael lay naked under the silken cover, his face still showing the traces of tension and pain. She crept into the bathroom and was quickly under the warm shower. Chilled as she was, the hot spray was agony and ecstasy on her skin, but gradually she felt herself relax — she had her darling Michael safe at last. Only now could she allow herself to acknowledge the extent of her terror when she had feared the worst.

She would stay here until morning. She could doze by the fire and slip away easily. Someone from the castle could come down to attend to him then, for he might not feel like seeing her.

Wrapping herself in his robe she made her way on tiptoe to the bedroom door. His eyes were closed, but he stirred when he heard her move.

"Julia?" He reached wearily for her hand, and she went towards him. "Stay with me, Julia. Please don't go away now." His voice drifted back into sleep as Julia struggled to force back tears. The sight of this powerful man, asleep like a vulnerable child before her, was overwhelming.

She felt no doubt. There was nothing else she could bear to do. The robe fell loose as she eased herself between the smooth sheets, propping herself high against the pillows. He sensed her presence, and, barely awake, he moved to rest his head on her breast. Even as she cradled him, he was sound asleep.

Julia leaned her head back against the soft pillows, no longer able to stifle her tears. She caressed his scarred cheek, stroked his hair, wondered at the sensation of his skin against hers. His body was relaxed against her, the powerful muscles slack. He was heavy but she welcomed the weight, protecting and cherishing him as he lay in her arms. "I love you, Michael," she whispered, her heart bursting with emotion. "I love you so much. Please, please love me!"

Although she was exhausted, Julia could not sleep. Several times, Michael stirred and she held her breath until he was asleep once more. Finally however, as the first light of dawn penetrated the room, she opened her eyes to find him looking at her.

"Julia . . ." She could barely hear his voice for the pounding of her own heart and, as he drew her towards him, slipping the robe from her shoulders, there was no going back, nor did sne want to.

At first, it seemed almost like a dream, his skin warm against hers, his arms strong around her. He kissed her eyelids, the lobes of her ears, the corners of her parted lips. His fingertips whispered sensually upon her breasts, her stomach, stroking, caressing, sending shivers of anticipation through her body.

But gradually his touch became more urgent and he pulled her more tightly to him. She found her body arching towards him, following his lightest touch, aching for more. She felt no shame in responding passionately to him, her desire sweeping her towards him, helpless yet secure in his embrace. His body was firm and hard against her and she sensed his need. He drew back the sheets, catching his breath at the sight of her.

"You are beautiful!" he groaned, almost as though in pain. He bent his head to her throbbing breasts, his lips teasing the nipples, sending shocks of agonised delight through her. His hands explored her body, her thighs, the taut muscles of her stomach, and she ached for more and more, silently begging him not to stop.

Innocent though she was she knew that

he was an incomparable lover, setting her alight with every touch. Feeding his own desire with hers, he fondled and caressed her limbs until she felt she would die of longing if he did not possess her completely.

As though sensing the overwhelming tide of her desire for him he finally moved over her body, his weight and strength lovingly dominating her as she surrendered joyfully to him. It seemed that she had waited so long, loving and wanting him, yet afraid. But she need not have feared his love; he came to her at last, reining his passion, taking her for his own with such gentleness that she felt only pleasure — reaching, soaring, until she was lost in ecstasy.

Returning to herself at last, she felt his body slack against hers. Now, she thought, I know what perfect happiness is. She felt completely at peace and, safe in his arms, she drifted into sleep.

She knew nothing until she woke to find herself alone. She lay still for a moment, trying to hold on to what had happened. She glowed with the memory.

The bathroom door opened, and Michael appeared, clad in a towel. Smiling lovingly at him, she was shocked to find him clearly avoiding her eyes. She sat up, gathering the sheet around her, her stomach churning.

"There are fresh towels in the bathroom," he announced, and at the unmistakable coldness of his voice, the warmth which had surrounded her evaporated. "When you've showered, there will be coffee in the kitchen before you leave." He began to dress, his back turned to her, and she staggered into the bathroom, her senses reeling, barely able to hold back the tears until she was out of his sight.

The blood screamed in her ears. It was unbelievable! Unbearable! At last he had made her think that he cared and now, in a matter of hours, he was like ice towards her. She stood in the shower, sobbing until her body shook with misery.

She could not face him. She had given him everything and still he was casting her aside. She was not ashamed, but she felt cheated, used. Dressing hastily, she left the Lodge, relieved that Michael was still in the kitchen and did not see her distress.

She managed to reach her room without encountering any of the staff but when she opened the door Anne was there, standing by the window.

"Julia! Thank goodness! Is he all right?"

Realising that Anne was still concerned primarily with Michael's condition after his hill-walking, she burst into hysterical giggling, which swiftly changed to heart-rending tears.

"Oh, Julia, what on earth is wrong?"

"I can't talk about it Anne, not now. Please, will you help me pack? You don't mind leaving early do you? I have to get away!"

Anne, true friend that she was, asked no questions. Following Julia's instructions, delivered with an unnatural calmness, she packed bags and cases. Julia splashed her face with cold water and put on some eye make-up as camouflage before going down-stairs to tell the staff that she had to leave for London earlier than expected. Thinking she had some domestic crisis to return to, they assured her they could cope easily until Robert's return.

Within two hours of her tearful return to the castle, she and Anne were climbing into a taxi with barely enough time to catch the noon ferry.

The haste with which their departure had been organised had, mercifully, left Julia no time to think about what had taken place. It was only as she stood on the forward deck, looking out towards the castle, that she felt a terrible weariness come over her. She was utterly drained by the emotions and events of the last twenty-four hours. Now, she felt like an escaped prisoner; relieved to be free, yet strangely afraid of the world to which she must now return.

What a fool she had been! How could she have believed that he loved her? After all, he was flesh and blood, and he had woken to find a naked woman in his bed. His natural reaction had not necessarily been a sign of true love.

"Chin up, girl!" Anne put a comforting arm around her shoulder. "I don't know what he said or did, but I'm sure no man under the sun is worth tearing yourself apart over."

"You don't even believe that while you're saying it," Julia laughed through her tears. "You're always rushing in where angels fear to tread!"

The gangway was pulled away and they watched as the ropes were cast loose. The engines roared as the ferry inched away from the pier. Suddenly the sound of a car horn blasting repeatedly startled those who stood waving on the pier and, to Julia's amazement and horror, the silver Mercedes screeched to a halt at the end of the pedestrians-only area.

He leaped from the car like a man possessed, yelling her name. Her face crimsoned as other passengers, and those who stood amazed on the pier, realised who he was and at whom he was shouting. Even the resolute Anne uttered a gasp of disbelief.

"Julia!" he shouted, as the ferry moved further away, "Julia, for God's sake! What are you doing, you idiot?"

She covered her eyes with one hand, gripping Anne's arm tightly with the other. But still Michael shouted and yelled, apparently oblivious to the crowds watching him in fascination.

"Julia Markman!" he bawled. "I'm sorry! Damn you, woman — I love you!"

Her fellow passengers were loving every minute of this! Not content with privately humiliating her, he had turned her into a public spectacle too. The final straw came when a voice nearby called her name and, as she turned, a photographer, obviously returning after covering Michael's social jamboree, snapped the vital picture. She turned on her heel and went into the ferry's lounge where she hid herself in the dimmest corner.

"You need a drink!" said Anne, appearing several minutes later, with a large brandy.

"Oh, Anne . . ." Julia tried to speak, but could not.

"Don't say a thing, love. Another hour and we'll be in my little car and homeward bound. Then you can forget all about this place and its lord and master."

EIGHT

For twenty-four hours after their return to Aunt Liz's flat Julia slept almost continuously. Only then did she feel able to face the world. She had poured out her story to Anne during their long drive home, begging her to tell Aunt Liz simply that a romance had gone wrong. Now, as she emerged from hiding, she was asked no questions, offered no unwanted advice, but she was aware of the warmth and protectiveness which surrounded her.

She was a strong and independent young woman, however, and soon her sense of her own worth reasserted itself. She still felt weak and bruised emotionally but she was determined that she would not allow anyone, not even the man she loved, to crush her spirit.

She had dealt with hurt in her life before, and she knew that it simply had to be lived through. So Anne was pleasantly surprised when, a few days later, Julia appeared fresh and smiling, if a little pale, and suggested a trip into the city to browse through the Autumn fashions. Although she had loved the tranquillity of Rosa, she had occasionally missed the hustle and bustle which had been part of her life in London and Paris.

The tiredness Julia felt that evening was the healthy exhaustion caused by tramping through shops and trying on every garment in sight! She had thoroughly enjoyed herself and if, occasionally, she had appraised a garment with Michael's reaction in mind, she had quickly steered her thoughts away.

Now, as they chatted over supper, the phone rang. It was Robert.

He talked cheerfully about his holiday, asked if she were enjoying hers. At first, it seemed that he did not know she had left Rosa under a huge cloud. But finally, after an awkward pause, he told her that Michael had left for London himself.

"He has a lot of business to tie up. I shouldn't be surprised if he contacts you."

"I'd really rather he didn't, Robert."

"Look Julia — I know how upset you are just now. But please remember. Whatever happens, Rosa will always be here for you, if you decide to come back to us. We all miss you!"

She murmured a reply and Robert wished her a happy holiday. He had been the soul of tact. Not wishing to confront her with what had happened he had, nevertheless, placed himself firmly on her side and she truly appreciated it.

It was on the following day that the gifts began to arrive. Julia was in her room when Anne tapped her door. "Er . . . Julia, I think you'd better come through here," she muttered mysteriously, and following her out into the hall Julia discovered an enormous bouquet of perfect red roses.

"Just delivered," Anne said in response to her cousin's wide-eyed disbelief. "There must be six dozen roses here — and no card!"

"How sweet of Robert," Julia replied, fixing her with a look intended to halt any further discussion.

But on the following day there was a box of handmade chocolates and, the day after that, a beautiful silk scarf.

Anne ventured to speak on the subject at last when she appeared with a package just delivered by hand from the city's finest bookshop. "It isn't Robert, is it?"

Julia looked at her, begging for help. "What on earth am I going to do? I can't go on accepting these things!" She unwrapped the package and discovered a beautifully illustrated book on porcelain.

"Porcelain?" queried Anne.

"It's a very long story. I must send this back."

"Should you? I mean, this is obviously the only way he has of apologising. Wouldn't it be rather unkind . . . ?"

"Unkind!" Julia exploded, and instantly regretted it. Anne was only trying to help. "Perhaps it is, but what does he expect? He's spent his whole life treating people like objects — and he's not going to do it with me! I won't give him the chance to hurt me again." At that moment, however, her eye lighted on the porcelain figure he had given her — an object. And her heart told her that he loved those porcelain figures.

"No!" she told herself. "I am not so fragile!"

But the daily arrival of gifts, large or small, ensured that she could not escape from thoughts of him, even if she left the package unopened on the hall table. Finally, realising that was exactly what he wanted, she grew angry and determined to put a stop to it. But how?

She was in the kitchen that evening when Aunt Liz called her to come and see the News. "It's about Lord Michael!" she said, as Julia moved in, expecting news of some international disaster. Over film clips of one of his racing triumphs, and a still photo of Michael himself, before his accident, there was a report that he had decided to sell his share in the team with which he raced. Various estimates were given of what he was worth and what this would mean to racing. An interview with him would be included in the programme which followed the news.

"Why on earth should he be selling up?" asked Anne.

"I have absolutely no idea," replied Julia, quite bewildered by the report. "Perhaps he is moving abroad? Honestly, I just don't know."

It was a curious experience to see him on the screen. He looked different, somehow, more sophisticated, even more handsome, and in a flirtatious mood which delighted the female interviewer who asked him about his decision to quit the world of racing. Was it because of his injury?

"Well — yes and no. While I was recovering at home, on Rosa, I had a lot of time to think. And I came to the conclusion that I wanted to settle down there, take over the running of the castle. My brother, Robert, will be heavily involved in agricultural development on Rosa, so there is a lot to do."

"Settle down? Does this mean we'll see less of the jet-setting Lord Michael? Is there marriage in the air?"

Michael smiled. "I have no comment to make on that."

"But the young lady pictured in the popular press?" Julia whirled to look at her cousin, whose face was bright with embarrassment.

"A misunderstanding on the photographer's part," Michael was saying. "Miss Markman is my mother's secretary. She was leaving Rosa for a short holiday and will be returning soon to work with me." Julia snapped the set off.

"Right! Which picture in the 'popular press'?"

"We didn't want you to be upset," protested Aunt Liz.

"You know what they're like, these papers," Anne was trying to sound casual.

"Show me!"

Shaking her head ruefully, Anne fetched a newspaper cutting. Here indeed was the photograph snatched on the ferry, of Julia, in obvious distress; and, worse still, the accompanying caption. 'Latest Love for Racing Lord?' 'Rumour has it that sizzling actress Kerrin O'Brienn has lost her place in the affections of racing aristo Lord Michael Muirisson, to an unknown London secretary. Miss Julia Markman (23) is seen here leaving Rosa, Lord Muirisson's Scottish isle, after a lover's tiff with the playboy Lord, but he has now followed her to London to patch up their differences!'

Julia's rage knew no bounds. Ignoring their attempts at calming her, she ripped the cutting to shreds. "Age 23! A 'secretary'! They can't even get their facts straight! How dare they do this to me?"

It was all very well for the likes of Kerrin to be treated like this. Publicity of any kind was food and drink to them but for Julia, who had always been a very private person, it was unbearable. She knew that gossip pages survived on the candy floss of such stories. Better and more famous young women than herself had been appallingly treated by hungry news-hounds bent on a story. But still she could not help being hurt by it all.

Such was her hurt and anger over the photograph and story that it was some time before she considered Michael's interview, and the implications of what he had said at last came home to her.

He was returning to Rosa, permanently.

He was going to run the castle, as Robert hoped. But what of her? He had claimed she would return to assist him, but he must know that that would be quite impossible? She would never be able to return now.

The telephone rang and was answered. Hearing the footsteps approach her room Julia wondered if the press was going to pursue her. She was almost relieved then, when Aunt Liz told her it was Kerrin O'Brienn.

"Julia?" Kerrin sounded quite friendly.

"Hello, Kerrin! How nice to hear from you." Julia knew she sounded brittle, but she could not imagine what the purpose of this call might be. She was wary, fearing that Kerrin would blame her for the story.

"I wondered if we might have lunch together tomorrow — or Friday? I have something I want to discuss with you."

"If it's about that silly article . . ."

"Goodness, dear, I'm delighted with the publicity! I've got a premiere coming up soon you know. And it's all grist to the mill."

"Well —" Julia was still hesitant, but finally agreed. She would go to Kerrin's flat. Wise to the ways of the media, the actress thought it better to keep their meeting private.

"You know, Julia, I am your friend," said

Kerrin, as though sensing Julia's doubts. "And I know that you and Michael belong together. 'Bye 'til tomorrow!" Having dropped her little bombshell of a comment, she rang off.

Julia was still doubtful as she emerged from the lift into the lushly carpeted hall outside Kerrin's flat. 'Don't be silly,' she told herself and, taking a deep breath, raised her hand to knock.

"Now don't be cross with Kerrin!" said Michael as he caught her wrist and pulled her inside.

"Cross!" She was about to detail her anger when his lips silenced her. Furious, she pulled away.

The expression on his face was so serious that instantly she regretted it. "Don't draw away from me like that, darling," he said quietly. "Please give me a chance to explain." He sat down and, clutching her handbag to her to emphasise that she would be leaving very soon, Julia sat too, at the opposite end of the corner suite, a discreet coffee table between them.

She looked down at her lap, trying to conceal her burning cheeks. She wished she could magically transport herself from here, escape from whatever was going on, but already he was talking, sounding so calm, so gentle, that she had to listen.

"I knew you'd never agree to see me — and I don't altogether blame you. Kerrin wanted to help, because she knows this is special. Julia — you can't know what I've been through since I met you!"

Her indignation was kindled. "What *you've* been through!" she gasped.

He was silent for a moment. "I've never loved anyone before. I never knew what the word meant. And it frightened me. Right from the start I knew this was different. Even on the terrace, I was just trying to scare myself off by treating you harshly, I couldn't admit what was happening, especially since I felt you might just be acting out of pity."

"Oh, Michael . . . !" Surely he must have known that she had loved him from the start?

"When Kerrin and the others came to Rosa, she saw immediately what I felt for you, even before I would admit it myself. But I told her she was crazy, she should know me better." Julia looked at him and could see from his expression that he believed what he was telling her.

He stood and came towards her, taking her hands in his. She tried to draw them away, she could not bear any more of this, but he held her firmly.

"You are going to listen to me, Julia," he said, his voice tense with determination. "This is far too important for us to play childish games." He dropped her hands. "I know you think I rejected you — after that night. But . . . Oh, God, how can I make you understand?" Abruptly, he walked towards the window, and stood looking out over the river.

Her heart thudding, Julia stood and went towards the door, but as she reached it he grabbed her arm and whirled her round to face him.

"I love you, Julia. You must believe me!"

"Goodbye, Michael," she said quietly, removing his hand. Her knees shaking, she walked to the lift. As its doors closed, she saw him still standing there.

Escaping into the busy streets outside, relieved that he had not followed her, she wandered for hours through store after store, trying to keep her thoughts from dwelling on Michael. But the latest obsessions of fashion — the layering of winter outfits, the matching of clothes to your underlying skin tone, the importance of owning a Wok — the triviality of these concerns angered her. Finally, as she sipped coffee from the tiny cup offered in a prestigious store's restaurant, she allowed her mind to travel to where it wanted to be. Could she, after all those previous incidents, trust him now? Could she ever forget him? Could she ever live without him?

It was late afternoon when she hailed a taxi for home, only to find herself giving Kerrin's address. He was right. This was no time for childish games, and the adult thing was to go back and hear him out.

But it was Kerrin herself who opened the door, and her face clouded when she saw Julia. "You'd better come in, I suppose," she murmured, grudgingly. "But if you're looking for Michael, he isn't here."

Julia sat down heavily, appalled at the sense of anti-climax. Kerrin brought her a drink, and thrust into her unwilling hand the scribbled note Michael had left.

Dear K. — You were wrong. She wouldn't listen, and how can I blame her? I'm going back to Rosa immediately. Will be in touch. Love & thanks M.

"Really Julia, what do you want of him?" Kerrin's protectiveness and anger on Michael's behalf shocked Julia out of her dazed state. "Can't you see that he really does love you? He really does. And it wasn't easy for him to admit that to himself, far less to you!"

Noticing the girl's wan face and seeing that she was close to tears, Kerrin relented and, sitting down by her side, she put an arm round Julia's shoulder, speaking more gently now.

"I am very fond of Michael, you know. But he has never loved me — never loved anyone until you, Julia. I care enough about him to want his happiness, so I'm telling you this as your friend and his — he adores you, and you plainly love him! What more could you possibly need?"

As she lay on her bed at home, trying to make some sense of her jumbled emotions Julia wondered if she was being too stubborn; using lack of trust as an excuse, when in fact she was childishly trying to pay back the pain he had caused her.

She decided to soak in a long, hot bath — an old remedy for a muddled brain. She moved quickly around the room, gathering her robe, talcum powder, make-up bag. Perhaps it was the sound of the running water, or tiredness, or anxiety which made her careless. She would never know. But suddenly, as though in slow motion, yet unstoppable, the precious porcelain figure — her gift from Michael — was toppling from its place on the dressing table to break into several pieces on the floor.

Less than twenty-four hours later she was standing once more on the deck of the Finnsport ferry, this time approaching Rosa, the jagged mountain peaks dark against the deepening purple of the autumn sky. She laughed aloud — she should have known she would return. This beautiful island was a part of her now, and its magic was far-reaching.

The taxi-driver recognised her immediately.

"Welcome home, Miss," he said warmly, and Julia thanked him. It was home for her now, and always would be if Michael still wanted her. "The Castle, Miss?"

"No, Jimmy. Take me directly to the Lodge, would you? No need for the rest of the family to know I'm back just yet." She whispered, as though letting him in on a secret.

"No problem, Miss!" He winked at her, so good-humouredly that Julia giggled at their conspiracy. After all, thanks to the national press, the whole island would be discussing her and Michael!

As so often before, there was no reply to her knock, but she opened the door so that

Jimmy could leave her luggage there before going off with a wicked twinkle in his eye. The house was empty, but a fire glowed in the huge ingle and she knew he could not be far away.

Turning up her collar against the cold she hurried back outside and, hoping her instinct was correct, made towards 'their' shore. As she emerged from the trees she could see him, much farther along the beach, gathering driftwood. She smiled, remembering the other times they had spent together on that shore.

"Michael!" she called, her voice trembling.

For the rest of her life she would cherish that moment when she saw recognition dawn upon him. Throwing the bundle of wood to the ground he began to run towards her and then, as though momentarily afraid that she was not real, but some crazy figment of his desperate imagination, he slowed to an urgent stride. She waited there, knowing such happiness that she wished this moment might last forever.

"Oh, Julia!" With one final stride, he gathered her into his arms, crushing her to him, smothering her upturned face with kisses, before his lips finally met hers. All the longing they had felt for one another found expression in that kiss.

"I love you, Michael, I love you," she sighed as he held her to him. "Take me home now."

Lying beside him on the rugs, in front of the glowing fire, she knew real joy. Nothing could separate them now. Their lives had become interwoven; they belonged together, as they belonged, also, to the island they both loved.

Their bodies were made for each other; each touch, each caress, a pure expression of their commitment one to the other. Where, before, there had been fear mixed with their physical passion, now there was only a feeling of the rightness of their love.

Finally, still holding her as though he could not bear to be separated from her even for an instant, Michael spoke. "I can hardly believe I have you here! I was so sure you did not believe me, that I had lost you forever. What finally brought you back, my darling?"

Julia nestled close against his chest, loving the warmth and strength of his body. She remembered yesterday's small tragedy. "I have a terrible confession to make. The porcelain figure you gave me — it's broken. I shouldn't think it could be repaired."

"Oh, that's not important now!"

"But it is," she interrupted, silencing him

with a gentle finger against the sensuous curve of his mouth. "It is important, because it was when I saw it lying there in pieces that I knew I must come to you. No matter how valuable it was, how difficult to replace, it was after all, an object, a thing." She clung close to him at the thought. "But our love, and the joy we could find together — how could I risk breaking that, when there could never be anyone in my life who could replace you?" Her voice quivering with emotion she lifted her gaze to look at him, and saw love mirrored in his eyes.

"Porcelain is fragile, Julia. Our love will be so strong that nothing will ever destroy it. Now, all I want is for you to be my wife, as soon as it can possibly be arranged. Then, everything I have will be yours."

"I don't know what kind of 'Lady' I'll make," Julia laughed, but Michael had the answer.

"Don't you remember the wonderful Duchess Louise? What did I say about her — ? 'An independent mind and great beauty'. A perfect description of you, my love!"

"Didn't you also describe it as a terrifying combination?" Julia teased.

"But as you know," he replied as he drew

her once more into his arms, "I am not easily terrified. And besides — I love you."